Everybody Loved Bridget

They all told her so. Frank, the brilliant composer who wanted Bridget to star in his opera. Mike, who was always ready to give her the money and the affection she needed. Peg, who nursed her back from the brink of death. The police, who had put a permanent guard on her person.

Who, then, had drugged her? Who had put the incriminating hypodermic in her room? Who had framed her on a charge of theft? Who had followed her on her desperate cross-country flight from Manhattan to a lonely ranch in Arizona?

And who now had her hopelessly, helplessly trapped. . . ?

sleep
without
morning

---

rae foley

a dell book

Published by
DELL PUBLISHING CO., INC.
1 Dag Hammarskjold Plaza
New York, New York 10017

Copyright © 1972 by Rae Foley

Dell ® TM 681510, Dell Publishing Co., Inc.
Reprinted by arrangement with
Dodd, Mead & Company
New York, New York 10016
Printed in the United States of America
First Dell printing—March 1973

For Jim Todd with affection

sleep without morning

1

The window rattled as a gust of wind struck it. The worst winter on record. The words drifted through Bridget Evans's mind. The worst winter on record. Sleet clawed at the pane and the window rattled again. Bridget listened to the storm in the detached drowsy state between sleeping and waking. She didn't want to wake up. She was afraid to wake up. While she lay like this, warm and safe in bed, the world shut out as long as her eyes were closed, her mind curtained by sleep, nothing could happen to her.

If only she did not ache so badly, if she were not so hot. Her skin seemed to be on fire and her chest felt raw when she tried to draw a deep breath. She began to cough, a long hacking cough that left her exhausted.

"So we are awake at last! How do we feel?"

Bridget was aware of the nurse who gave her a bright professional smile. Through the open door of the small room, she heard the tinkle of covered dishes as small trolleys laden with breakfast trays were being pushed past, aware of hushed voices, of purposeful footsteps, of a pervasive medicinal smell.

"Where—" she began urgently, and she did not recognize the hoarse rasping voice as hers. Before she could utter another syllable a thermometer was thrust under her tongue. The nurse took her wrist in a red, scrubbed hand and looked at her watch.

"No!" There was something Bridget had to do. Something she had to do at once. Something—she had been running in the snow; she had slipped on ice almost under a taxicab. But why was she doing it? What had happened to her? Something horrible. And how long ago had it been? She remembered that she had been in a frantic hurry because—because—and then she remembered all of it.

She jerked the thermometer out of her mouth and sat up. "What day is this?" Her voice rasped and she coughed again.

"No, no," protested the nurse, alarmed by her manner, by the pulse that leaped and jerked and raced under her finger. "That's no way to act. Lie down and—"

"What day is this?" Bridget's voice rose. It had been three o'clock in the afternoon when she had run into the street. It was morning now.

"Monday."

"Where am I?"

"If you'll just lie down, I'll call your doctor," the nurse said, aware that this was something she could not handle by herself.

"For God's sake, answer me!"

"You're in a hospital. A taxi driver struck you, and he brought you here. We couldn't notify your family because you didn't have any identification on you, nothing but a key and a handkerchief in your coat pocket. You can't trust anyone these days. I suppose the cabbie stole your handbag."

"You suppose wrong. I didn't have a handbag, and he wasn't to blame." Again Bridget was racked by a cough and confused by the hoarse voice that was not hers. "I was running," she went on when she could speak again, "and slipped and fell. I'm lucky he didn't run over me."

"What on earth were you doing out in a snowstorm without boots and with your coat unfastened? I undressed you when you were brought in. Your dress and shoes were sopping. Enough to give you pneumonia."

"I was trying to find a policeman." Bridget attempted to pull herself upright on her pillow though her head was stabbed with pain as she moved and there was a moment when everything blurred. "Look here," and there was urgency in her voice, "I've got to speak to a policeman at once. Two whole days lost!"

"Now, now," and the nurse was firm, "you have a concussion and a fever. Just take it easy. Everything will be fine."

"Fine," Bridget repeated. "Oh, dear God!"

"And when you've had your breakfast—"

"I've got to see a policeman if I have to go out and find one myself."

The nurse laughed. "Without your clothes?"

"If necessary."

She would, too, the nurse thought, watching the girl's flushed face uneasily. No one had told her this was a mental case, so perhaps it was a head injury or delirium. "What do you want with a policeman?" she asked, trying to sound reasonable in the face of an unreasonable demand.

"I've got to report a murder. That's why I was running. I was looking for a policeman."

"You saw a murder?" The nurse was skeptical.

"And the murderer. Every minute you waste gives him that much more time to get away."

The nurse touched the burning skin, saw the parched

lips, the fever-bright eyes, felt the rapid, uneven pulse. "Well, I don't know—"

"Will you or won't you get me a policeman?" Bridget said between set teeth.

"Wait a minute." The nurse went out of the room, disturbed but excited.

Bridget began to cough again, a fit that left her limp and exhausted. She was no longer aware of the wind raging outside the window or the snow that fell like a heavy curtain or the distant sound of horns muffled by the storm. She saw a woman slumped in a chair, staring at her with bulging sightless eyes, her tongue projecting from her mouth as though making a monstrous face, a noose embedded in her neck.

After a time a young intern came in to ask her name and address and to take her temperature and pulse. He listened to her chest and back with a stethoscope and made hasty notes.

"I've got to get up," she told him frantically.

"If you don't lie down and behave yourself," he told her, "you won't be allowed to talk to anyone." Somewhat to his surprise, for he was a very young intern, she obeyed the voice of authority and slid meekly under the blanket.

"I'll do anything you ask if you'll just call the police," she said, her voice a hoarse whisper. "Please! Please! A woman has been murdered. Every minute lost helps her killer to escape."

"All right." The doctor looked down at her. Not more than twenty-one with large dark eyes and short dark hair, a small straight nose and full lower lip, heavy lids and a stubborn jaw. She was trouble incarnate. She would carry trouble with her wherever she went, as Typhoid Mary carried disease, but that kind of trouble would be easy to take if a man was will-

ing to live dangerously. The intern had no objection
to a little danger.

She turned her head on the pillow, wincing with
pain. "What's wrong with me?"

"A concussion, not serious but painful, and acute
bronchitis."

"How long will I have to stay here?"

"Well, you need bed rest and medication; perhaps
you can go in three or four days."

"And how long before you call that policeman?"

"Okay, lady. Keep your cool. We'll get one for you."

She watched him leave the room and lay with her
eyes fixed on the open door. In a few minutes a policeman would come in, a policeman who might or might
not believe her. But this time it was she who had called
the police. That ought to count in her favor. Or would
it?

On the whole she still did not know, after she had
told her story to a noncommittal plainclothes detective,
how much he believed. The interview had not gone at
all as she had expected.

"My name is Carmichael," he said from the doorway.
"You got anything contagious?"

She shook her head in surprise. "Concussion and
bronchitis," she managed to say, her voice rasping.

Reassured, he came to lay his snow-covered overcoat on a chair, put his muffler and gloves and hat on
top of it, and draw up a chair beside the bed. They examined each other frankly. He was in his middle thir-
ties, she thought, with flat cheeks and thin brown hair,
the tip of his nose still reddened by the January winds.
He pulled out a handkerchief, blew his nose, and
then inhaled deeply, one nostril at a time, from a
small tube, which he returned to his pocket. Then he
drew out a notebook and a pen. If a house was burn-

ing down, she thought in exasperation, he probably would go through the same deliberate routine before he called the fire department.

Name? Bridget Evans. Address? 1502 West Fifty-second Street. Occupation? Singer. Well, actually, a music student.

"They said you wanted to talk about a murder."

"It was Saturday afternoon, about three o'clock. I went to see a friend of mine, Mrs. Elizabeth Conway, who has a penthouse in the block across from Carnegie Hall. When I got out of the elevator, there was a man leaving the penthouse. He was a very large, young man, perhaps six-foot-three, and he weighed about 230 pounds. He had a fair complexion, a big nose, not like Cyrano but quite a beak. He was wearing a gray suit and a blue necktie and a heavy, lined raincoat, the kind you get in Scotland. He was about twenty-five years old. He passed me and got in the elevator. I rang Mrs. Conway's bell several times and then called. It made me uneasy when there was no answer, because I was sure Liz was expecting me, so I went in. Liz—Mrs. Conway—was in her music room, and she had been strangled. There was a noose around her neck."

Carmichael thought she was not going to say anything more. Then with an effort she went on. "I tried to get it off but I couldn't, and I shouted for help. Then I remembered that Isabella, her maid, had been given a few days to visit her family in New Jersey; so there was no one in the penthouse, and Liz doesn't—she didn't have a telephone. So I had to go for help. The lobby—it's an office building with no apartments—except for the one Liz had—is always deserted on Saturday afternoons; so I started to run across the street, and I slipped and—" Her hands clenched on the blanket. "That's all I know. But Liz—all this time—and he'll get away."

Carmichael looked at his notes. "The girl at the desk told me that you were thoroughly chilled when you were brought in, your coat was unfastened and you were wearing no boots."

"I forgot them."

"You knew that your friend was dead?"

"Oh, yes. Oh, God, yes!"

"Then you could not help her in any way by so much haste, could you? There was nothing to be lost by taking a few moments to put on your boots and button up your coat."

Bridget looked at him in bewilderment. "I didn't think of anything but Liz. The shock—and she looked so horrible—and I wanted—before the man got clear away—"

"Oh, yes, the large, young man. You had never seen him before?"

Bridget shook her head and felt pain lance through it.

"Did you feel that he was upset or excited? Was he startled when he saw you?"

"I don't know. I wasn't paying much attention to him."

"And yet you noticed even the color of his necktie and his hair. In fact you observed quite a lot for a fleeting glance."

"Well, I—" Bridget broke off, confused, obscurely alarmed by the detective's manner. "I don't see—"

"What I am getting at is this, Miss Evans. You were calm and collected enough on your arrival to notice a great deal about a strange, young man whom you saw only briefly, but when you left the penthouse to go out into one of the worst storms we've had this season, you forgot your boots."

"But I had just seen the best friend I have in the world after she had been brutally murdered."

"You must have been in a real panic to rush off without fastening your coat or taking your boots."

"What in heaven's name have my boots to do with it?" Bridget exclaimed in irritation.

"You say you're a singer. Singers don't take chances with their voices; they don't risk catching cold."

Recalling his manner when he had entered the room, Bridget retorted, "It's a cinch you don't take chances. I suppose if a criminal had a common cold, you'd let him go rather than catch it." Then she groped toward his meaning, her mind slowed by fever. "You mean that I killed Liz and then panicked and tried to run away and fell—and when I was brought here and couldn't get away I—invented the large young man. Is that it?" Her voice rose almost to a scream, and a passing nurse stopped to look in the room. Carmichael went to speak to her in a low tone, murmur an explanation, and flash his badge.

He shut the door and came back to resume his seat, studying Bridget. She had plenty of what it took to attract men if she cared to use it; so why did she act as though they were her natural enemies? Or was it just the police? She behaved as though she had had some unpleasant encounter with them, though you couldn't always tell, with all the stuff handed out by malcontents and neurotics about fuzz and pigs.

"You say that this Mrs. Conway was a great friend of yours?"

"She was wonderful. When I lost my job and had no more money to pay for my singing lessons, Madame Woolf asked her to hear me sing, and she not only promised to pay for my lessons but also to finance my debut and she—oh, built up my confidence."

"You couldn't pay for your own lessons?"

She shook her head.

"No family?"

"My father died a year ago and left me a small life insurance policy, because he didn't think I could be trusted with money." Carmichael's eyelids flickered and he bent over his notebook. "So I got a part-time job and then I lost it—"

"Why?"

The girl's expression altered. There was defiance in her face, or was it fear? "What has that to do with Liz?"

Something in her attitude alerted him. "Can you give me the address of your former employer?"

"Why should I?"

"Why shouldn't you?"

"Because, if you knew your job, you'd be looking for the large, young man instead of asking me ridiculous questions."

"Oh, yes, the young man who was right on the spot. What made you so sure that he killed her?"

"He was coming out of the apartment when I got there and he could not have failed to see her as soon as he went inside. The door of the music room was wide open. And if he was innocent he would never have gone away as he did, without a single word. He wouldn't have let me go in—unprepared. Decent people don't act like that. Innocent men don't run away from murder. If you'd stop bothering about me and why I forgot my boots and think about him—"

She was really something when she was excited, Carmichael thought. Disturbingly attractive. Pint-size dynamite. Pity she was a liar. She'd be causing trouble as long as she lived, which was the conclusion the intern had reached, but Carmichael had no inclination to live dangerously. He encountered all the trouble he wanted in the course of a day's work without having to look for any. And a girl who would take the attitude she had adopted, said he was afraid of a common cold—you couldn't expect any man to put up with anything like that. Gave you a real insight into the girl's character.

The door opened, and a middle-aged man with a tired face came into the room, a stethoscope hanging around his neck. He put his hand on Bridget's wrist. "The patient should not be receiving visitors, particularly at this hour. Regular visiting hours are from two to four and seven to nine; that is, if she is able to see anyone today. You'd better telephone and inquire first."

"I represent the police."

The doctor was not impressed. "I represent the hospital. This patient has a fever and she is not to be questioned any further at this time. I refuse to let her be disturbed."

Carmichael shut his notebook with an air of finality. "That's all—for now, Miss Evans."

"If I can think of anything useful I'll get in touch with you."

"That won't be necessary. We'll keep in touch with you," the detective said gently. "Be seeing you, Miss Evans."

2

News of Mrs. Elizabeth Conway's murder broke in the afternoon papers and on radio and television. The brutal strangling of a wealthy and famous woman in a penthouse was a natural, and the news media were making the most of it, digging up stories about the eccentric woman who had met so ugly a death.

Lieutenant Baxter of Homicide looked with distaste at the container of coffee—as usual they had put too much cream in it, making it a pale and unappetizing color—and the sandwiches wrapped in wax paper. He had just come from Mrs. Conway's penthouse, leaving behind him a corps of experienced men. The body had been photographed, drawn, fingerprinted, and removed for autopsy hours before. There had been no time for dinner.

Baxter drank some of the coffee and read the account of the murder in the evening paper before turning to his reports. The case was going to be a little stinker. Not a clue so far. Not a hint of a motive. They'd have the press driving them crazy and he'd be the one to have to stall them. The inspector liked to hand out statements about new developments and an early arrest in which no one believed. Baxter saw no sense in that. He told them as much as he was permitted to and let it go at that. It would have surprised the inspector to know that hardened newspapermen were inclined to put far more reliance on any statement of Baxter's than on most public pronouncements. When he could tell them the truth, he did so. He did not fall back on the politician's method of appearing to say a great deal while saying nothing at all.

Across the desk Sergeant Carmichael carefully measured out six drops of yellow liquid into a teaspoon. He had a sensitive stomach and he should not have to eat his meals at irregular hours. He drank a glass of milk and read the account of the Conway killing. Just as he might have expected: he had been the one to report the murder but there was no mention of his name. Everyone else in the department got his name in the papers. Come to think of it, there was no mention of the Evans girl or of the large, young man. His story had been ignored as usual. Baxter was up to his tricks again, making sure that Carmichael was kept out of the limelight.

Carmichael belched and covered his mouth politely. Lieutenant Baxter scowled in irritation as the sergeant's stomach rumbled. Whenever Carmichael was aggrieved, he developed indigestion. The man was a hypochondriac and, worse than that, he went through life with a sense of ill-usage. He didn't have what it took to get ahead in the department but he was disgruntled when other men were promoted over him. Men with a grievance could be troublemakers, and, though Baxter had not yet learned how much of a troublemaker Carmichael could be, he was tempted to have him transferred to another department where he would become someone else's headache.

For over two years the lieutenant had tried, patiently at first, then with increasing exasperation and acrimony, to teach Carmichael to respect facts, but he could not pride himself on his success. The sergeant always developed a theory of his own, fell in love with it, and doggedly tried to make the facts fit it like the Procrustean bed.

Carmichael put down the newspaper and coughed as though trying to attract attention.

"Well?" Baxter asked shortly.

"There's no mention of the Evans girl in this account." What the sergeant meant was that there was no mention of him, but he could not quite bring himself to say so and face Baxter's ironic eyes.

"Well?"

"I suppose you have your reasons. It's obvious to me the girl killed the woman herself and then panicked and ran." He went to the drinking fountain and came back with a paper cup, unscrewed a bottle, and solemnly shook out a couple of pills. "This indigestion. Nothing seems to work."

"If," Baxter said irritably, "you would put as much thought on your job as you do on your insides you would get somewhere. Maybe. I'm warning you, Carmichael, that you need something better than symptoms on your record. Something a lot better."

"Yes, sir. But I don't see how I'm going to get anything on my record this way."

"Oh?" Baxter was not encouraging.

Carmichael swallowed. He might as well go through with it now. Nothing ventured. "Well, I brought you the Evans girl's story and her tall tale about the large, young man and there's not a word about it in the paper."

"That's right." Baxter's manner was a warning that Carmichael did not heed.

"I suppose you're afraid of tipping off this guy. Well, I can tell you for a fact he doesn't exist. The girl gave him to us as a nice fat red herring. She's guilty, Lieutenant. She's a liar. Why she didn't even expect me to believe her! If you ask me, she's been in trouble with the police before and I'm going to run down her record."

"You do that."

"She lied," Carmichael repeated stubbornly. "She told me she was going to look for a policeman, and she forgot to put on her boots before she ran out into the storm."

"Well, what about it?"

"She is a singer, Lieutenant. A singer thinks first about her voice. She doesn't risk catching cold. I have a cousin who sings in a church choir and she spends half her time spraying her throat."

"My God! Perhaps it runs in families."

Carmichael held on to his temper. Could he help it if he had always been delicate? Always the first to catch any disease and always to have it the longest and the hardest. "If that girl forgot her boots, it was because she was in a blind panic. She was running away. We would never have heard of the murder from her or of the large, young man if she hadn't knocked herself out and landed in the hospital."

"Have you discovered her motive?" Baxter asked politely.

"Yes, I think I have. She admits herself that her father left her nothing but a small life insurance policy because he thought she was not to be trusted with money, and she was dead broke at the time when Mrs. Conway agreed to pay for her music lessons. In other words, she'd have had to give up her career without Mrs. Conway's help. But suppose Mrs. Conway found out something about the girl, something in her past—"

As Baxter cleared his throat, Carmichael rushed on. "Wait, Lieutenant, it makes sense. The girl got fired from the job she was holding, and she refuses to say why or tell me who her employer was. Something wrong there. And if Mrs. Conway found out about it and refused to give her any further help—"

"If—if—if—" Baxter's fist crashed unexpectedly down on the desk. "Get me some facts. Facts, man! I don't want any more theories. Theories don't look well on your record."

There was a curious flicker in Carmichael's eyes, he started to speak and then reached out to silence the telephone. "It's for you. A Mr. Field who says he was Mrs. Conway's lawyer."

"Good." Baxter talked briefly. "He's coming in. Seems to be greatly upset about the Conway murder. Apparently she was an old friend as well as his client." The lieutenant watched sourly while Carmichael settled down to type a report. Then he opened the scanty file on his desk, looking at the pictures of the woman with the noose around her neck, and went over again Carmichael's account of his talk with Bridget Evans. He wondered fleetingly about the large young man. Killer or red herring? And the girl who had forgotten her boots. Baxter grinned. Poor Carmichael with his obsession with health. He was getting to be a damned nuisance. Now he wanted to get his name in the papers. He'd do better to pay more attention to what got on his record.

A policeman came into the room ushering a slight man of fifty-five, with heavy white hair above a narrow face and an air of boundless energy, subdued at the moment by shock. "Mr. Field, Lieutenant."

II

"Everyone loved Liz," Field said.

"So everyone loved her," commented the lieutenant. "The fact remains that she died with her head in a noose." Even in his well-fitting gray suit, he was obviously a policeman. It was in the carriage of his head, the searching look in his eyes, his hard mouth, and the speech that had been pruned down to essentials. He was well-trained, well-disciplined, and, as he prided himself, an honest cop. It was not his intention to be brutal, though he lacked imagination. You can't spend fifteen years in the homicide division of a great city police force and come up with any rosy illusions about human nature. He simply called the shots as he saw them.

The man across the desk winced at the picture that had been evoked but his only comment was the mild question, "Haven't you discovered anything? It was nearly forty-eight hours since she died."

"But we discovered her death only this morning, you know."

The lieutenant was accustomed to facing hysterical or distraught relations; it was a relief to deal with the victim's lawyer, a controlled man who, for all his avowed devotion to his dead client, could be relied on for common sense and some practical assistance. Leonard Field, of Field, Warburton, and Wells, was the head of a distinguished legal firm. The fact that he had voluntarily come in person to put himself at the disposal of the police was an indication of the esteem in which he had held his late client and his determination that her murderer should be found. He was not, Baxter noticed in relief, the kind who would throw his weight around or drop casual if menacing hints about how well he knew the commissioner, but he wouldn't miss anything, and he would be on them like an avalanche if he found them sitting on their hands.

"I would like the full account, please." It was a request and not an order. Field opened a notebook and took a pen from his pocket.

"Well, as you know, we discovered Mrs. Conway's body about ten o'clock in the morning. She was sitting in a chair in her music room. Are you familiar with the penthouse?"

The lawyer nodded.

"There was a noose around her neck. There were no signs of a struggle. She had not been molested sexually. Nothing had been disturbed. Nothing seems to have been stolen. She was wearing a valuable solitaire diamond, and there were eighty dollars in her billfold, which was in plain sight on a dressing table in her bedroom. So we have to eliminate a sex angle and theft. Her maid, who returned tonight from visiting relations in New Jersey, collapsed with shock and what appeared to be quite genuine grief and had to be put under sedation."

"A number of people are feeling quite genuine grief." Field's voice was dry.

"So it appears. Of course, we haven't had much time to look into her circle of friends, but Mrs. Conway seems to have had no enemies. All the people we have been able to reach say, as you say, 'Everyone loved Liz.' We can't find the smell of a motive, and we don't even know how the killer got in, unless Mrs. Conway admitted him—or her. There are no signs of a struggle, and you can't have a physical tussle without leaving some traces of it—overturned furniture or something of the sort—and Mrs. Conway's clothing was not in the least disarranged, not a hair out of place. She had obviously been sitting quietly in the chair when that noose was slipped over her head."

Field was silent for a while and Baxter did not attempt to hurry him. "Just what is being done, Lieutenant?"

Baxter found himself on the defensive, not for his own sake but for the department, though Field's question was raised quietly enough.

"Quite a lot has been done in the time we have had. You understand, Mr. Field, the police are doing everything possible. The medical examiner has already set the approximate time of death at two to four o'clock Saturday afternoon, based on the food contents in her stomach. We aren't overlooking any bets. The penthouse has been gone over for fingerprints, for all the good that will do, but we have to go through the motions. There are prints all over the place, particularly in the music room. As luck would have it, Mrs. Conway gave a small musical party the night before, thirty guests to hear a string quartet she was planning to launch."

He broke off to digress. "It's a funny thing. They seem to have had a deep regard for her, but all four men have been at me, wondering whether this destroys their chances to have their appearance at Town Hall paid for."

"Liz helped a great many people and most of them needed cash to make a debut."

"Yes, well, as I say, the music room hasn't even been dusted, so it's hopeless to get anything meaningful from prints in a setup like that."

Baxter turned pages. "Of course, we have been questioning all thirty guests, now that we've got the list from the maid. It's a long job and probably won't give us a thing. People don't observe what is right under their noses, and they get confused when they are questioned, change their minds and their stories or don't remember. It's maddening, but there you are."

"Anyhow," Field pointed out, "the party was held on Friday evening, and she must have been killed sometime Saturday afternoon. I don't see what bearing—"

"I told you we aren't overlooking any bets. Reaching far out, maybe. We're casting a wide net because so far we simply haven't unearthed the smell of a motive for her murder. She appears to have been a kindly, generous woman—no rumors of any quarrels or ill will. The last person, you would think, to attract violence. We're digging for any information—any gossip—" He lifted his hand in a gesture of helplessness and let it drop on the desk again.

Field was not a man to waste words, probably because he had to listen to so many of them in the course of the day. "How may I help you?"

"Had you known Mrs. Conway long?"

"Twenty-five years, both as her lawyer and as a friend, and that, I think, is an important clue to Liz Conway. Whatever your relationship with her might be, you inevitably became her friend."

"Tell me what you know about her. The reason for her death must lie somewhere in her life."

Elizabeth Conway, Field said, had had a brilliant but unfortunately brief career as a contralto in Wagnerian roles, cut short by a thyroid operation. She married Jonas Conway, a well-to-do industrialist, but she had never been satisfied to limit herself to the empty life of a society woman, and her adoring husband was content to let her follow her own inclinations.

"I don't know what it was about Liz. She wasn't beautiful by any standards and not even moderately good looking. She was big and robust as a Wagnerian singer must be, careless about her personal appearance and casual about her surroundings."

The lieutenant nodded. "I noticed the clutter in the music room, with sheet music and records and signed photographs piled on the piano and record player, on shelves and chairs and even on the floor."

"Cluttered but comfortable," Field assured him. "I never felt more comfortable anywhere than in that room. I can remember how shocked her friends were when she moved into an office building in the West Fifties with shops on the street floor and offices above. Some of her friends never got over their horror at the cigar stand in the lobby. But no one could have cared less about an unfashionable address. Liz wanted the place because it was so close to Carnegie Hall that she could walk there in all seasons regardless of weather. As you must have discovered, there is a private elevator to the roof. Very few tenants in that building knew of the existence of the penthouse so that she had more privacy in a way than she could have had in a regular apartment building with the conventional sort of lobby and doorman and all that. She didn't care about," he groped for the word he needed, "the trimmings."

Baxter shook a cigarette out of a package. "That building has been one of our major problems. From our point of view, it couldn't have been more unfortunate, particularly as the murder occurred on Saturday afternoon when offices were closed, the cigar stand in the lobby had been shut down, and the only operator on duty was helping to repair a stalled freight elevator in the basement. We haven't found a single witness who saw anyone use the roof elevator all afternoon. A dozen people could have come and gone unobserved, and, of course, Mrs. Conway's only servant was, most unfortunately, out of the city."

"Liz didn't have servants; she had help. Of course, while Jonas was alive, she had a larger staff; but Isabella Morente came to her years ago as her dresser while she was still in opera, and then she stayed on to rule the roost—and Liz—as a benevolent despot. Of course, Liz could have lived more luxuriously though not more comfortably—she had a real talent for comfort—but she said she had other uses for her money."

"Which brings me to the chief question I have to ask you. How much money did Mrs. Conway have to dispose of, and who gets it?"

"I brought the will with me. She had rather a lot of money and property. Here are the figures, and I believe they are complete; it is a substantial estate and soundly invested."

"What are the main provisions, without the 'whereases'?"

For the first time during the interview, Field's eyes glinted with laughter. "There are no 'whereases.' The will was drawn the way she wanted it, with just enough legal phraseology to protect her wishes. It's a highly characteristic document. Music was her abiding passion, and, when she lost her own career, she devoted herself without bitterness to helping young music students get a start. The bulk of the estate goes to the Juilliard Foundation in New York, the Curtis Institute in Philadelphia, and the New England Conservatory of Music in Boston for scholarships with the warning: 'Don't you dare lower your standards!' "

"Well, it's a cinch that no institution put that noose around her neck," Baxter said bluntly.

"There are only three personal bequests. One has

29

been in the will since I first drew it up for her after Jonas died: ten thousand dollars to Isabella Morente, referred to as 'my faithful friend.' "

"There's no possibility that the maid—the help—killed Mrs. Conway. We have found half a dozen people in New Jersey who testify that she was there at the time of the murder."

"It never occurred to me to suspect Isabella." The lawyer consulted his notes. "There is one question mark, if you like. Ten days ago Liz added a codicil to her will, leaving fifty thousand dollars to her husband's niece, Simone Marguerite Daumier, with the comment, 'You should have told me long ago. It's high time to forget old grudges.' "

"Grudges! What was that all about."

"I don't really know." Field saw the lieutenant's skeptical expression and smiled. "I really don't know, beyond the fact that Jonas disapproved of his sister's marriage to some Frenchman; she was hot-tempered and hot-headed and never forgave him, and I don't believe he ever saw her again. Apparently he was justified in his opinion of Daumier who was a drifter and never supported his wife and child. I gather the poor woman had a tough time making ends meet. Liz didn't tell me much; I think she felt badly because Jonas had let his disapproval prevent him from helping his sister. I don't know how Liz ever discovered the niece's existence, but I do know she was considerably upset about the whole situation. The way she saw it, she was living in luxury while her husband's sister and her child were in want. I know she planned to see the girl." The lawyer forestalled the next question. "Whether she did or not, I have no way of knowing. The day she initialed the codicil in her will was the last time I ever saw her."

"Anything else?"

"Yes, a legacy of the same amount, fifty thousand, to a young music student, a protégée of hers, named Bridget Evans, 'to help you remember it's only the future that counts and to launch you professionally. You'll make them sit up and take notice, Bridget, but that's the hell of a name for an opera singer.' "

"Well!" The lieutenant seemed to have taken on a new lease on life, and Sergeant Carmichael sat up with a jerk, his eyes gleaming with satisfaction. "Well, well. There is one thing that didn't get into the newspaper account of Mrs. Conway's murder and that was how we got on to it in the first place. A young woman named Bridget Evans called the police this morning—she is in a hospital with a concussion and had been unconscious until then—to say she had found the body of Mrs. Conway Saturday afternoon about three, saw the murderer leaving the penthouse, and she was running for help when she skidded almost under a taxicab."

Field's eyes raked the lieutenant's unrevealing face. "Apparently you don't believe her story. Why?"

"Not at all. I haven't talked to the young woman myself. Sergeant Carmichael here saw her. He didn't believe her. He believed—"

"I believed she was the killer," Carmichael said.

"Could she have managed it?" Field's voice was steady, though he was obviously shocked.

"You mean physically? Oh, yes. The noose was a piece of ordinary clothesline with a slipknot. All that was necessary was to get behind her, drop the noose over her head, and yank hard. It would not require a great deal of strength, and it wouldn't," Carmichael added hastily, seeing Field's sick expression, "take long. The pressure on the—"

"I know." Field looked at Baxter. "Do you credit this theory? What was supposed to be the girl's motive? Liz was extremely fond of her and she was financing her career."

Baxter nodded to Carmichael. Let the man have his hour in the spotlight; it might clear up his indigestion.

"I believe there is something in her past that Evans was afraid Mrs. Conway would find out or perhaps had found out. Something to do with the cause of her father's distrust of her and with some job she had lost. She was hostile and refused to discuss it. And, as for the large young man—" Carmichael repeated the girl's story.

Baxter broke in to ask Field, "Do you know of any man who would fit that description?"

Field shook his head.

"Have you met the girl?"

"I have never seen her but Liz spoke of her frequently. According to her, Miss Evans had had a bad break of some sort. Liz was vague about it."

"She probably didn't know what it was," Carmichael said, and Field eyed him curiously, wondering at the strength of the man's prejudice against the girl.

"I wonder if she knew she was down for fifty thousand," Baxter said.

"I don't know but my own guess would be that Liz didn't tell her. She was one of those rare people who dislike being thanked."

"And the other chief legatee, the niece," Baxter said. "Can you tell me how to reach her?"

Field shook his head. "Liz had a phenomenal memory and she never needed an address book."

"What about telephone numbers?"

"You must have noticed that the only telephone in the penthouse was in the kitchen, for Isabella's convenience. I doubt if even Liz's oldest friends knew of its existence. She said that having a telephone was like keeping open house all the time."

"I suppose the best way to smoke out the girl is to give the story of the will to the news media. That ought to bring her running. No one is going to risk passing up fifty thousand."

Field looked at his watch. "If there is nothing else, I have a busy schedule tomorrow, and there are some papers I'd like to go over."

Lieutenant Baxter picked up a pencil and prodded his desk blotter with it. "What gets me, Mr. Field, is that everyone says the same things about Mrs. Conway. As a rule, even the best of friends see different qualities in a person or are aware of some shortcomings. But the testimony about her is all of a piece."

"Well?" There was an unstressed challenge in the lawyer's voice.

"Well, it may all be true, but it's the first time in my experience that I have encountered a human being who never made a single enemy, who never even aroused dislike or resentment because of envy or jealousy or a sense of grievance of some sort. It just isn't natural. You must know that from your own dealings with legal clients. All we've got is Mrs. Conway's own comment about old grudges."

Field, who had pushed back his chair, hesitated, and then seated himself once more. "Actually, there was such a case some weeks ago." As Baxter brightened he shook his head. "It couldn't have had anything to do with Liz's murder—just an isolated and pointless tragedy. What happened was this: a young girl committed suicide and left a note blaming Liz Conway. She claimed she could have been a second Beverly Sills if it hadn't been that Liz ruthlessly destroyed her chances in order to advance Bridget Evans. The papers played it up because of Liz's prominence and her news value, so I got in touch with her at once. She flatly refused to make any public statement to exonerate herself from any responsibility for the tragedy, but she told me privately that the girl couldn't sing for sour apples and she would never have been able to have a career in music. She had come to Liz to ask her help, and, after hearing her sing, Liz had turned her down as gently as she could. Unfortunately the Evans girl was there at the time and was getting the red-carpet treatment. Naturally Liz was upset about the suicide, though she was sensible enough to know the charge was ridiculous and she was not in the least to blame. I think she disliked it chiefly because of the involvement of Miss Evans. For some reason she had a protective feeling about her."

"I don't remember the case," Baxter admitted. "I'll look it up. What was the girl's name?"

"It's an odd name, Snodgrass, Louisa Virgilia Snodgrass, but there was nothing in it for the homicide department. A clear verdict of suicide—no doubt at all. The girl's father, a timid, defeated little man, claimed the body. He said his daughter had been displaying some paranoid tendencies, and he had been worried about what she might do, as she was subject to attacks of violence. In fact, I suspect he was relieved in a way that she had killed herself rather than injured someone else. He blamed himself, in fact. He said he would never have married if he had known his wife's medical history, and the condition had not shown up in either of his children until they were adolescents. His wife is now in an institution, and he is keeping a close watch on his son."

"Good God! But Snodgrass doesn't sound like the vengeful type."

"Oh, no. Not at all. I called on him at Liz's request because she wanted to pay for the funeral. He refused; he said it was his responsibility, but he was grateful. Surprised and grateful. A nice little man."

3

"Later," Lucy Graves said firmly. "Later. You can tell us all about it, but right now you are too upset. Mike, hurry up with those cocktails."

The tall young man grinned. "To hear is to obey."

Leonard Field leaned back in the big comfortable chair, watching with a sense of idle well-being while his hostess bent to touch a match to the Cape Cod lighter and send a blue flame licking around the birch logs in the fireplace. She straightened up, a tall slim woman with a dramatic streak of white in her black hair, a narrow vivid face with the kind of skin that remains almost unlined well into old age. She wore a black dress with a crimson scarf fastened on one shoulder by a diamond brooch, an indication that she had left off mourning for her husband, and inwardly Leonard Field rejoiced. He had loved her for years and he intended to marry her.

He heard the pleasant sound of ice against the pitcher and Michael Graves brought frosted glasses, which he filled. The lawyer thought that he would enjoy having Mike for a stepson. He had never been misled by Mike's indolent manner. Anyone, who, at twenty-eight, had acquired a reputation and an impressive income with a series of television plays that were neither soap opera nor horse opera, that were witty and designed to appeal to the informed intelligence, had something on the ball. If Mike had been warned that television programs are created for junior high school mentality, he had never let it deflect him from his course, and his success had justified him in the eyes of the self-appointed Cassandras who had assured him that it could not be done.

Field sipped the chilled martini slowly, watching the blazing logs through half-closed eyes, content with the moment. Then his hostess aroused him from his state of euphoria by setting down her glass with a soft tinkle. "It's all right to rest," she exclaimed in exasperation, "but there's no sense in overdoing it. I want to know what happened when you saw the police last night. There hasn't been anything new in the papers today."

Mike laughed. "My dear little old mother is simply bursting with the usual womanly curiosity, Lenny."

"Of course I am," she admitted.

"They are going through the motions. That's about all. So far as I can tell, they haven't learned anything new since I talked to Baxter. Liz was strangled with a noose slipped over her head. She wasn't assaulted sexually; she wasn't robbed; there is no indication of a struggle. Apparently she admitted the killer herself, and that means it was someone whom she had expected because she never consented to see strangers unless they had written her for an appointment."

"Then there are no clues? Not a single solitary clue?" Lucy asked.

"Just trifles," her son assured her. "Prints of a bare foot on the ceiling, scraps of a letter in code, a stocking mask—"

The sight of the lawyer's drawn, unhappy face made Lucy say with unaccustomed sharpness, "That's not funny, Mike."

"Sorry," he agreed at once. "That was rotten taste."

"Actually," Field said, "the police aren't telling all they know, not by a long shot. There's a lot of routine, checking fingerprints, checking on friends and acquaintances, reaching far out, as the lieutenant said, and, by the way, I'd take him for a highly competent man. There's just nothing to get hold of. It's incredible that anyone should have wanted to injure her."

Mike stretched his legs toward the fire, turned the cocktail glass in long fingers. "Look here, Lenny, let's leave the matter of clues to the experts. That's their province—like fingerprints and checking alibis—and all that. But you knew Mrs. Conway well. When a woman like that is brutally murdered, and that noose meant premeditation, there has to be a powerful reason. Take away sex and theft and what motives are there: revenge, fear, profit. And who profits, by the way?"

"That's what Lieutenant Baxter wanted to know." Field repeated the gist of the will.

"Of course, the foundations are out. That leaves the three legatees: the maid, the protégée, and the niece."

"It wasn't Isabella." Field was firm about that. "She had been with Liz for many years and she adored her; anyhow the police have established beyond doubt that she was in New Jersey at the crucial time; half a dozen people saw her there."

"Then what about this Bridget Evans? If Mrs. Conway said, 'It's only the future that counts,' it means the girl had a past, doesn't it?"

Field shrugged. "Liz was always vague about the girl's past."

Lucy Graves looked at him quickly. "You were this woman's friend as well as her lawyer for a quarter of a century and yet you expect me to believe you didn't take any steps to learn anything about that protégée? Don't be absurd, Lenny. You don't function that way."

"Liz wouldn't have liked any interference on my part."

"But just the same—"

Field laughed outright as he saw her eager expression. "All right then. I checked, simply as a precaution. All I could find was that Bridget Evans came from Connecticut; her father had been fairly well off but he left her only a three-thousand-dollar life insurance policy. Everything else went to his housekeeper in gratitude for the care she had taken of his daughter." The lawyer held out his glass for a refill. "The girl did not attempt to contest the will."

"He only does it to annoy because he knows it teases," Lucy explained to her son.

"Actually, I'm not holding anything back. For some reason Evans neither liked nor trusted his daughter. After his death she came to New York, using the insurance policy to live on and got a part-time job to pay for singing lessons. She was fired from her job without a recommendation and told her singing teacher she would have to quit. It was Madame Woolf, her teacher, who came to Liz and asked her to hear the girl. Liz was enthusiastic and took over the expense of the lessons and, I am inclined to think, though I have no proof, did a lot for her—clothes and all that."

"And now she rakes in a cool fifty thousand," Mike said thoughtfully.

"I doubt if she ever knew about the legacy, and, in any case, unless she were desperate, she would not have risked sacrificing Liz's immediate help. Liz carried a tremendous amount of weight in music circles."

"How desperate?" Mike asked.

"Suppose," Lucy commented, "Mrs. Conway had learned something to her discredit, would she have stopped helping her?"

"If I had had any answers, I'd have produced them at the police station."

"Well, what about the niece?" Mike asked. "What about those old grudges? How old? How big a grudge?"

"Don't ask me. Apparently the girl's mother had a rough time—perhaps real hardship—certainly a serious financial problem. How bitter would the girl be? The idea that her uncle's wife was living in luxury while her mother was impoverished might lead a badly balanced person to violence, but I must say it sounds more like some of your dubious fiction."

Mike grinned at him amiably. "I resent that."

"And you aren't to use any part of Liz's life or death as material for one of your plays."

"Mike wouldn't do that," his mother said indignantly. "In some ways the boy has quite nice instincts."

"You unman me," her son said in a broken voice. He went on briskly, "Well, sex is out; theft is out; profit— according to Lenny—is unlikely. That leaves revenge. Any candidates except, possibly, the niece?"

Field repeated the story of Louisa Virgilia Snodgrass who had committed suicide and of the note she had left. "Nothing there, I am afraid. The father is a most inoffensive man. The mother is in an institution. Apparently the son lives with the father."

"Does anyone know where he was at the time Mrs. Conway was murdered?"

Field shrugged. "I suppose it would be wise to find out. The police never knew of any connection between Liz and the Snodgrass case until I told them last night."

"There was no mention of it in the paper this morning either."

"There's a good deal that wasn't in the paper," Field said and told them of Bridget Evans's call to the police, her report of the murder, and her description of the large young man.

"And you waited all this time to tell us!" Lucy said indignantly.

"The man from the homicide division who interviewed the girl believes she was lying. In fact, he believes she killed Liz and invented the man."

"But your lieutenant didn't give that story to the press," Mike said. "Why not?"

"Baxter is no fool, Mike. He has a sound reason for what he does. And if we assume that the girl is telling the truth, she'd be in the hell of a spot if the story came out. How long do you think the large, young man would let her remain free to identify him?"

"But he knew she saw him."

"He didn't know who she is or where she lives."

"Does anyone know what the Snodgrass son looks like?"

"But why would he kill Liz?"

"If he blamed her for the destruction of his sister's career."

"You like to go out on a limb, don't you? Is this the way you construct one of your plots?"

Mike grinned. "Always start with 'just suppose' and take it from there."

"Well one thing is sure," Field said. "Either the Evans girl is guilty and in danger of arrest or she is innocent and in danger from the murderer, at least if that story ever gets in the news."

Mike glanced at his watch and went to switch a news station on the radio.

"Today a major break came in the Conway murder case," said a brisk voice, "when Sergeant James Carmichael of the homicide division of the New York police force gave us his personal account of the discovery of the murder. Miss Bridget Evans, a young music student residing at 1502 West Fifty-second Street, Manhattan, told Carmichael that she not only discovered the body of Mrs. Conway but that she also saw the killer just as he was making his escape from the penthouse." A description of the large, young man followed.

"Miss Evans claims to have entered the penthouse at three o'clock Saturday afternoon where she saw the murderer leaving and found the body of her friend. In panic haste she rushed from the apartment, tried to summon help, and fell on the ice outside the building. She was knocked unconscious and taken to the Methodist Hospital.

"The contents of Mrs. Conway's will were later divulged by her lawyer Leonard Field, of Field, Warburton and Wells, who described it as a highly characteristic document. Miss Evans was left a legacy of fifty thousand dollars and another fifty thousand goes to a niece of Mrs. Conway's husband, 'to help her forget old grudges.'

"The homicide department, according to Sergeant James Carmichael, is hard at work on the case and expects to make an arrest in the immediate future."

Mike shut off the brisk voice. "The fat is in the fire. If I were Bridget Evans I would dig myself a hole and pull it in on top of me."

"If she is innocent," Field agreed. "I'm surprised at Baxter, allowing the sergeant to make such a statement."

Lucy leaned forward, bringing her slim hands together in a quick gesture. "Lenny, why don't you let

Mike take a look at the Evans girl? He could get more out of her than the police; he could find out whether she is guilty or in danger—"

"Where I get this gruesome reputation for being an authority on women," Mike began, "I can't imagine. And of all the unscrupulous people I know, my dear old mother—"

Field did not share Mike's amusement. "Liz was devoted to this girl. On that account alone I shouldn't like to think of anything happening to her—if she is in the clear, if she really had no part in Liz's death. Are you serious, Lucy, about Mike trying his hand with the girl?"

"Of course I am. He has always yearned to be a knight-errant."

"The hell I have!" Mike was revolted by this picture of himself.

"Anyhow, the police aren't doing much, Mike, and Lenny is worried about his old friend's murder and this girl is—at least she may be—a sitting duck if she can identify a man who may be a murderer."

"Or just possibly she may be a murderer herself," Mike reminded his mother. "That is the main thing."

"The main thing," Field said heavily, "and one that is in danger of being lost sight of, is that someone murdered Liz, and her killer is walking around right now, as free as air, free to come and go as he pleases or to kill again if he pleases. Do you have the time and the inclination to take a look at the girl and see what you make of her? I'd appreciate it. If she murdered Liz I want her to pay for it; if she is innocent, I want her protected for Liz's sake."

"Please do," Lucy said.

Something about their implicit faith in him made Mike laugh in some embarrassment. "Unto the breach, dear friends. Also dying I salute you. Or something."

II

The brisk voice said, "The homicide department, according to Sergeant James Carmichael, is hard at work on the case and expects to make an arrest in the immediate future."

Lieutenant Baxter shut off the radio and looked grimly at Sergeant Carmichael. The latter, carefully measuring out six drops of liquid into a teaspoon, wore the look of the cat at the cream saucer. He swallowed the medicine and washed it down with a cupful of water from the cooler. Then he look triumphantly at Baxter.

"You said I needed something on my record. Everyone but me gets his name in the news."

"And since when have sergeants given out stories for publication?"

Still unaware of the storm brewing over his head, Carmichael said happily, "I figured it might give me a better image in the department."

The veins in Baxter's face swelled, and Carmichael was uneasily aware that he had blundered or that Baxter was going to try to take away his triumph. Probably wanted all the credit to himself. It had been his story, hadn't it? If he hadn't told the reporter himself, no one would ever have heard of Carmichael, and the reporter had lived up to his promise and given him a nice play, a real nice play, using his name several times and even giving it in full. He had a right to stand up for his interests but Baxter was going to be down on him again. He knew the signs and it was going to upset his digestion.

It did. By the time the storm had broken, Carmichael was left white and shaking. A policeman halted for a

moment in the doorway of the small cubbyhole office
and then moved away on cat feet. Carmichael would be
left without an inch of skin on his back, he reflected,
without feeling any pain. Carmichael was not popular
in the department. He was suspected of holding back
bits of vital information until he could present them
with the most credit to himself, though police work is
teamwork; there's no place for a loner.

Nonetheless, much of Baxter's thundering rage broke
ineffectually over Carmichael, protected as he was by
an innate sense of his own righteous behavior and his
ill-usage. But he knew that once more there would be
nothing helpful on his record. And he shouldn't have
eaten that corned beef and cabbage for lunch; he
wasn't going to be able to digest it. But even his con-
venient habit of being able to shut out anything he
did not want to hear could not prevent him from hearing Baxter's shouted question, "What about the girl?"

"What girl?"

Baxter regained his self-control with a visible effort.
"I'm talking about the girl who claims that she can
identify a killer. You've put the finger on her. Would
you like to see your wife in such a spot?"

"I'm not married."

"That doesn't surprise me. Some woman is to be
warmly congratulated. You get a man up there to guard
Miss Evans until she is discharged from the hospital.
She is not to see any visitors or to be released until
some arrangement can be made for her protection. A
dead witness is of no use to us."

Carmichael swallowed. "I released that story just to
put the girl off the track, so she wouldn't know she was
suspected, so she'd think we believed that stuff about the
man she claimed to see."

"Oh, get the hell out! You ought to be walking a beat in Flatbush, and, if anything happens to her, that's what you will be doing."

"Yes, sir. But just the same, that girl was a liar. I could tell."

"That must be a new experience for you."

The sergeant's stomach rumbled. No wonder, with Baxter needling him all the time. "Her story was full of holes. She——"

"Get on the job and get someone to the hospital to keep an eye on her. If anything happens to her, I'll break you."

Carmichael swelled with the injustice of it but he answered, "I'll have someone at the hospital in a quarter of an hour."

Which would have been all right if Bridget Evans had not left half an hour earlier.

III

There wasn't, the harassed hospital authorities told the irate Baxter, any way they could have kept the girl there by main force. She had told them rather tartly that, not being Onassis, she couldn't afford hospital charges. Then she had dressed and walked out of the building where she had hailed a taxi. There were always taxis waiting at the hospital.

No, of course, she was in no condition to leave. She had a concussion, a fever of 103, and acute bronchitis. She needed bed rest and medication to clear the bronchial passages and there was always the danger that acute bronchitis would develop into pneumonia. She had been thoroughly chilled when she was brought into the hospital.

"So she's out on her own without a guard or any

protection," the infuriated lieutenant told Carmichael, who seemed to have shrunk.

Carmichael opened his lips, closed them again. You couldn't argue with Baxter when he was on a rampage. He reached in relief for the telephone, anything to escape temporarily from the storm of abuse he'd been taking.

"It's Mr. Field. He wants to ask you about my— about the news story on the Conway case."

Baxter studied the unhappy face of his subordinate in some satisfaction. "I should think he would." He identified himself, listened, glaring at Carmichael. "Well, of course, the story should never have been released. This man—if he exists—knows that the girl can identify him, knows who she is and where she is. . . . Naturally we thought of that, but our man Carmichael," and he kept accusing eyes on the unhappy sergeant, "was too slow. She had already left the hospital. . . . I assume she went home. We're checking there at once. . . . You have what? . . . You say this friend of yours has volunteered to keep an eye on her? . . . Well, as a rule, we prefer . . . No, I'm sure we can rely on your judgment, but I must insist that he take no steps without consulting me first."

The lieutenant lighted a cigarette and saw that Carmichael had pulled a small tube from his pocket and was snuffing up one nostril. He closed his eyes to shut out the sight.

"No, not at all. On the whole, Mr. Field, I'm glad to know that someone will be keeping an eye on her. We never have enough men. . . . Well, naturally, if any large, young man with a big nose puts in an appearance, I'd rather like to be informed. . . .

"Of course, there's always a chance the girl is in jeopardy because she claims that she can identify a killer, which is never a healthy occupation. . . . Yes, there's the Snodgrass character too. No, we haven't dug up anything yet. . . . Good luck to it, Mr. Field."

IV

"Today a major break came in the Conway murder case." When the broadcast had ended, the girl caught her breath, the color draining out of her face. "I could kill her for that."

"Don't panic. There's some way out. There has to be."

"What chance will either of us have?"

"We'll think of something."

"It had better be good," she said grimly.

V

"Today a major break came in the Conway murder case."

The man who had been listening shrugged his shoulders. He began to whistle, not jubilantly, but thoughtfully. It was an unexpected complication, of course, but it might even be useful.

VI

"Today a major break . . ."

Fifty thousand dollars. Nice work. Very nice work. And nothing to do for it. Some people really get the breaks. It was a sign, he thought, a lucky sign.

4

Bridget Evans huddled in a corner of the taxi, shivering, looking at the curtain of snow that cut down visibility so that traffic was crawling.

The driver had turned the transistor radio on, and she heard it unheeding until she was electrified by the words, "Today a major break came in the Conway murder case." She listened, her hands clenched on her lap.

"Oh, baby," the driver said. "Fifty thousand smackers! Nice work if you can get it." He added thoughtfully, "I wonder if the girl knew. Make a will when you have that kind of dough and you might as well cut your throat."

I didn't mean to. I didn't mean to. The sour taste of sickness welled up in Bridget's throat.

The taxi started, stopped again. The fresh snow had not yet become blackened by traffic film and it gave the street a certain spuriously festive quality, like Christmas decorations. Even in an age of conformity, Manhattan streets were widely unlike: Park Avenue and Second Avenue, Forty-second Street and Fourteenth Street— each one remained a separate entity with its own atmosphere and its own kind of people.

Bridget's world was limited to a small radius from Town Hall to Lincoln Center, but the part she knew best was Fifty-seventh Street, with its core at Carnegie Hall, a shabby building with placards announcing coming attractions. The glitter of Lincoln Center has not yet dimmed Carnegie Hall in the eyes of the faithful, who people the stage with ghostly figures of the musicians of the past and hear echoes of great music in the hall. Even the subway kiosk on the corner is unlike others, with copies of the *Musical Courier* more prominently displayed than the usual women's magazines and the so-called comics.

Above the stores and the restaurants, many of the buildings house the classes of ballet instructors and music teachers, but, of all the buildings, the noisiest is an old-fashioned, inconvenient building with drab and drafty halls and a creaking elevator which shakes its way up and down, that houses teachers of voice, piano, strings, wood winds, and brasses. On the top floor there are rooms for music students who not only live but practice there—an activity not encouraged by most landlords.

From eight in the morning until eight at night lessons are given and students practice. At any time bass voices can be heard thundering out their yearning to be tender apple blossoms, pianists work indefatigably on Bach fugues, and violinists assay the dizzying pyrotechnics of Paganini caprices.

Most of them work and dream of the debut on which their future depends, and, if many of them nourish unfounded dreams of an appearance before a cheering audience that would make the debut of Heifetz seem like a child's recital before doting parents, they are, after all, young and hardworking and, for the most part, talented.

"You'll have to wait," Bridget told the driver, "until

I can get some money to pay you."

He gave her a hard, suspicious look and then settled back with a surly nod, lighting a cigarette.

As usual, the opening of the inner door from the vestibule, with its little pools of dirty water from melting snow, unleashed a fury of discordant sound. A soprano was learning how to hit her top notes squarely instead, as an irate teacher was saying, of creeping up on them like a thief in the night. A clarinetist was tossing off golden phrases of Mozart, linked sweetness long drawn out.

The rickety elevator was standing open, and the operator was sitting on a stone bench outside, drinking coffee. "Hello, Bridget! Gosh, am I glad to see you! Ma was going to report you missing if you didn't show up by tonight, and then we heard this broadcast that's been on every hour saying that you were in the hospital and that you found Mrs. Conway's body. That must have been tough. And did you know she left you a—"

"Lend me three dollars, Giuseppi. My taxi is waiting."

"Living high on the hog, aren't you, taking cabs even before you collect your inheritance?" He hauled out a battered billfold and extracted three one-dollar bills. "Lucky Ma didn't get this first; she must of overlooked it."

As this was a standing joke, Bridget smiled obligingly and went to pay her relieved driver.

When she got into the rickety elevator, she said, "Tell Ma I'm home, will you?"

"Hey," he said in concern, "you're croaking like nothing human and your feet are wet. Where are your boots? You change your shoes and stockings as soon as you get upstairs. When did you leave the hospital?"

"Just now."

"Judging by the way you look you should have stayed there."

"I couldn't afford it." Bridget sagged against the wall of the elevator. Her head was swimming and lancing pains shot through it when she moved. Her eyes burned, her legs felt like cooked macaroni, and she wondered how they could hold her up without folding.

"I'd better ask Ma to come up and take a look at you." Giuseppi was genuinely worried.

Ma Baccante provided board for the students who occupied the top floor of the building. She also provided motherly advice, technical criticism, and an endless discussion of music. Her son Enzo was in the chorus at the Met, her husband played a viola in the orchestra, and Giuseppi played a church organ. To Ma Baccante, music was the only sensible way of life, and she nourished a dark suspicion that the American system had been threatened at its very core by the playing of guitars; when they took to amplifiers, she was assured that the end of civilization was in sight.

"I'm glad you're back for more reasons than one," Giuseppi said. "Now maybe that guy who's so sappy about you will cool down. He's been after Ma to go to the police ever since you failed to come home from your lesson on Saturday." He grinned. "You've sure got him hooked." As a racking cough shook Bridget, he said in alarm, "You go right to bed. Ma will send you up a bowl of soup. And be careful not to strain your voice. Madame Woolf would be screaming her head off if she heard you."

The community bathroom was empty, and Bridget took a long hot bath and then slept for a couple of hours. At last she forced herself to get up and dress. Several times she had to pause while she was brushing her hair because her arms were so tired. Through the walls she heard the Bach Toccata and Fugue in D Minor being played in the next room. Saul was doing some last-minute warming up for his Town Hall debut.

Bridget stared at her fever-flushed face and glittering eyes. She would be all right tomorrow. She had to be all right. She had already missed one lesson and she could not afford to miss another.

As she opened her door, the young man who had been leaning against the wall came away from it in a hurry, his face lighting in relief. "Bridget!"

"Hello, Frank." The husky voice was barely more than a whisper.

"Don't talk. You're straining your voice," he said anxiously, and, for the first time since she had awakened in the hospital, some of the horror and tension seemed to drain out, leaving her with a sense of comfort. Frank Saunders, from the day he appeared at Ma Baccante's boarding house, had surrounded her with an unobtrusive devotion; he accompanied her where he could, never insisting but always there when wanted. In contrast with the more flamboyant music students, he was low-voiced and quiet, with a boyish manner that endeared him to everyone, though he had eyes only for Bridget and seemed, indeed, to be unaware of the girls who vied for his attention.

When the elevator door opened, Giuseppi grinned. "I thought it wouldn't take Frank long to find you, but Ma will give you hell for this." He opened the door on the dark basement where Ma Baccante presided over a round table covered by a red cloth, with dishes of breadsticks and grated cheese. Bridget was the last to put in an appearance and she slipped into her chair with a croaking, "Hi."

There was a confused chorus of greetings: "I thought

you were in the hospital. . . . Did you know you've been on radio every hour with the news? . . . Did you really find poor Mrs. Conway? . . . Did you actually see her murderer? . . . Did you know she left you a lot of money?" Something in the girl's strained expression stopped the chorus.

Ma Baccante—she was Ma to everyone and put her boarders on a first-name basis at once—was an enormous woman with a round and unexpectedly youthful face for the mother of two grown sons. She came to smother the girl against her imposing bosom, exhaling garlic and affection. "Bridget, you should be in bed. Giuseppi told me you looked like a plucked chicken. I don't like to see my students"—they were always "my students" to Ma—"in that shape. You're no credit to my cooking and that's a fact. Just remember, it takes more than a voice to make a singer." She struck her breast. "It takes a healthy body; it takes lungs; it takes breath." She set a steaming bowl of minestrone before Bridget. "Get that down and go to bed where you belong."

"I'm going to Saul's debut."

The pale young man who was crumbling a breadstick managed a nervous smile. "Nice of you but you'd better do what Ma says."

"No," Bridget insisted, "I want to deputize for Liz. She would have been there tonight if she—could." Her voice wavered.

Ma broke the awkward silence by saying, "We've got some new members of the family, Bridget. Peg Reston. Mike Graves."

Peg was a big girl with red hair, green eyes, and freckles thickly scattered over a plain face, which was made attractive by a warm transforming smile. There was an air of repose about her. Mike was a casual man with an amused mouth and lazy eyes.

"Bridget," Ma explained to the newcomers, "is a coloratura soprano, though you wouldn't think there could be much voice in such a pint-size. At least she'll be cute as a button in *The Tales of Hoffman* and *Daughter of the Regiment* and the *Barber*."

"Comic roles," Bridget croaked gloomily. "Why not as Adèle in the *Fledermaus?*"

"Well, why not? Light music can be good music. You ask me and I'll say Mozart wrote better music when he was comic than in some of the symphonies. Don't downgrade music with laughter in it."

"Like Haydn," Saul said, emerging from his self-absorption for a moment.

"Beethoven had laughs in his music," put in one of the music students.

"But not wit. Just belly laughs."

"I suppose," Ma said severely to Bridget, "you are dreaming of *Norma*. Now you aren't Sutherland and you never will be, but you'll be fine in your own class if you stop straining your voice the way you are doing right now."

Saul pushed back his chair. "I've got to change. Mrs. Conway got me my evening clothes." He went away looking like a man walking the last mile, followed by calls of "Good luck. We'll be in the fourth row, rooting for you."

Mike spoke to Bridget for the first time as Saul got in the elevator. "Is he any good?"

"He is going to be one of the great ones. His technique is dazzling. Why he can rival Horowitz for sheer virtuosity right now."

Mike's expressive eyebrows shot up. "You are very generous. I thought most musicians were jealous of each other."

Bridget managed a smile. "Perhaps I'd feel differently if I played the piano. But I hope not."

The other newcomer, Peg Reston, turned to Bridget. "Did Mrs. Conway really arrange for his debut?"

Bridget nodded. "She was always helping students. She was—wonderful."

"I wonder," Frank said, "how many people she really did help."

"No one is likely to know. She didn't publicize her—"

"Charities?" Peg prompted.

"No, they were never that. Kindnesses."

"In a way," Peg said, "she was responsible for all my troubles."

"Liz!" There was protest and disbelief in Bridget's voice.

Peg laughed. "Not intentionally, of course, but I had all her recordings, and nothing would do but that I was going to be a Wagnerian too; so I went to Germany to study. That was my mistake. I just didn't have what it takes for that sustained kind of singing; so now I'll have to settle for Verdi, I suppose. You found Mrs. Conway, didn't you?"

Bridget nodded, swallowed, and pushed away her plate.

"I know how you must feel about it." Peg's voice was warm with sympathy.

"No one knows how I feel about it." Bridget was aware that Frank was watching her with anxiety in his kind eyes, and the newcomer, Mike Graves, was studying her intently. His was not a look of admiration, and she noticed that Frank was annoyed by it.

Peg was the only one attempting to talk. "Was the story on the radio right? Did you really see the man who—killed her?"

Bridget nodded. She did not try to speak.

"But you didn't actually see him do it."

"Good heavens, no!"

"Then how could you be so sure? He may have been just an innocent bystander."

"If he was innocent why didn't he report to the police? He was coming out of the penthouse when I saw him. He left the door open, which is how I was able to get in. He simply couldn't have helped seeing Liz if he as much as stepped inside. The door of the music room was wide open and she was in plain sight." The words rasped her throat though she was talking just above a whisper.

"But why," Peg began, "would anyone kill a woman like Mrs. Conway, unless there's a lot about her that never got in the news."

Bridget was dimly aware that the room was darkening before her eyes, and then she was sliding forward. Both Frank and Mike were beside her before she fell.

"I'll take her," Frank said in a tone that admitted of no denial, and Mike stood back so he could lift the girl in his arms. "Do you know a doctor who pays house calls?"

Ma did and lumbered off to telephone.

"I'll go up with her," Peg offered. "I'm used to simple home nursing. I can keep an eye on her tonight, in any case."

Frank, with Giuseppi's help—for some reason he refused to allow Mike to take any hand—put Bridget on her bed and Peg undressed her. Ma's tame doctor arrived to say she had bronchial pneumonia and that she must go to the hospital.

Bridget summoned up all her energy to say, as clearly as she could, "I can't afford it."

So Bridget slept and awakened, not always sure what was reality and what was troubled dreams. The image of

Liz haunted her. Now and then Sergeant Carmichael stalked through the mixed-up pictures in her mind, making skeptical comments and frightening her. Now and then she confused the plainclothes detective with a policeman in uniform. They had one thing in common. Neither of them believed her. Once the large young man chased her out of the sunlight and into a dark place where she was trapped by a wall and could run no more. Once she faced the Snodgrass girl, young and desperate, staring at her with accusing eyes, when Liz escorted her to the door.

Occasionally she was aware that Peg was lifting her on her pillows, spooning food into her mouth, giving her a cooling alcohol bath. Her movements were deft and gentle and she refused to let Bridget speak. A very restful person, Peg Reston.

And one night, Bridget, who had slept a good part of the day, awakened to see Peg Reston going through her handbag and her bureau drawers, the shaded light of a lamp on her red hair, her face intent, a face that was stripped of its kindness. And that, too, she believed later to have been a part of her delirium, because, after all, it could not have happened.

5

"I don't know," Mike said over the telephone. "At this point the girl is so ill there's been no possibility of conducting any personal research, but I can say this: she knows something she isn't telling and it's got her scared as hell."

"You really think there's a chance she is guilty?" Leonard Field sounded distressed.

"A chance, of course, but a slim one. I hope not. She's one hell of a girl. A knockout. I'd be willing to swear, by the way, there was a large young man, that she didn't invent him. She actually saw him."

"But if she suspects this fellow how can she be guilty?"

"She feels guilty about something, but I can't see her as a killer. There's something convincing about her gratitude toward Mrs. Conway. At the faintest hint of criticism, she is up in arms."

"That could be smart psychology."

"Perhaps."

"What are you planning to do, Mike?"

"I'll stay on here at Ma Baccante's boardinghouse for the time being. I think Miss Evans is safe enough right now because she is too ill to leave her room, and one of the music students is looking after her; also she has got herself a devoted admirer, a watchdog who hardly lets anyone near her."

At something in his voice, Leonard Field's eyebrows shot up in amusement. It sounded as though the unimpressionable Mike was undergoing a bout of jealousy. Then his amusement faded. He didn't want Mike involved with a girl of this kind. He made the mistake of saying so.

"What kind?" Mike asked gently, and Field made no reply, telling himself that he should have known better. "I'll keep in touch." Mike broke the connection, feeling vaguely annoyed with the lawyer and his implied criticism of Bridget Evans and his own instant resentment.

He stopped to consider his next move. For the time being the girl was safe because she was being looked after by the red-headed Peg Reston who struck him as being a competent person, not apt to be rattled or easily upset. A good dependable sort of woman.

The obvious next step was to get a line on Bridget Evans's background. Mrs. Conway's telephone number was unlisted; even Leonard Field did not have it; so Mike, his hat pulled low over his head, chin sunk in a wool muffler around his throat, trudged along the snow-covered, windswept street to the building where she had had her penthouse.

The maid, Isabella Morente, refused to open the door when he rang the bell, shouting that she wouldn't let in any murderers, and if he didn't go away, she would call the police.

He explained patiently, though feeling like a fool to be yelling through a locked door, that all he wanted was to talk to her about Mrs. Conway's young friend, Bridget Evans.

"And have that poor lamb killed too?" At the top of her voice Isabella called, "Help! Police!"

Mike ran for the elevator, half expecting to find the police awaiting him when he went through the lobby. There were only a few dim lights burning; the cigar stand was dark and deserted, and the night operator sat in a chair tilted back against the wall with the *Daily News* in an untidy heap beside him, working a crossword puzzle. He watched Mike cross the lobby, eyes intent. A murder in the building did not add to his sense of confidence.

Mike paused to speak to him. "Were you on duty Saturday afternoon when Mrs. Conway was murdered?"

"The police told me not to talk," the operator said. "I'm not talking."

"I only wanted to ask you—"

"I'm not talking. See? Out!" As Mike hesitated, he said, "There's a cop on the corner. If you want to ask questions, I'll call him."

"Okay, okay." Mike admitted defeat and went out, his shoulders hunched against the driving snow, sloshing through melting snow over a grating. There were few pedestrians on the street, and such as there were walked as quickly as was compatible with safety, eager to find shelter.

The lobby of Carnegie Hall was brightly lighted and crowded when Mike stepped in out of the wind to check the address on East Seventeenth Street given him by Leonard Field. As it was too late to drive to Connecticut and try to track down the girl's past, he might get a look at the Snodgrass setup. The young suicide provided the only evidence of hostility to Mrs. Conway, except for the missing niece, of course, and Mike had no clue as to the latter's whereabouts.

He ran for the subway, went down the damp steps to the platform, bought a token, and was lucky enough to board a local train almost immediately. At this time of night, there were only half a dozen people in the car, some of them reading paperback books, some of them dozing, all of them cold and uncomfortable, their wet coats steaming.

At Fourteenth Street, he climbed stairs and went out into the biting, bitter air. The address was a run-down apartment building east of Third Avenue. A baby carriage took up most of the space in the small entrance hall. In the dim light he had difficulty in making out the names over the mailboxes, some of them ragged, some indecipherable, some fly-specked, some ill-written. There was no Gustav Snodgrass, and Mike checked the address for the second time before he rang the bell marked "Superintendent."

He had rung twice more, and he was stamping his feet to keep warm and wondering what his next move should be when the door opened and an elderly man wearing a heavy sweater over flannel pajamas, glasses pushed up on his forehead, opened the inner door.

"You the superintendent?"

"Yes, are you looking for an apartment? We have a nice six-room apartment on the top floor, mostly furnished, rugs and curtains, four beds and some chairs and kitchen stuff. Kettles and dishes, all that, and bedding. A sublet and a real bargain." His voice was that of a cultivated man.

"Actually," Mike said, "I was looking for a man named Snodgrass, Gustav Snodgrass. I thought he was a tenant here."

"Oh, well, you're too late."

"How's that?"

"That's his apartment, the one I have to sublet. He's gone."

"Gone? Dead?"

"Oh, no, he moved out. He paid his rent in full up to

the first of next month." The old man shivered. "Cold as hell out here."

"May I come in and talk to you?"

The tired eyes brightened not only at the request but at the courtesy with which it was made. "Oh, of course. I was just about to make myself a hot rum punch and it's much more enjoyable to share it."

"Just the thing," Mike agreed. Having summed up his man, he put away the billfold he had taken out. The old man was offering hospitality and not expecting a tip.

The superintendent's apartment was in the basement and surprisingly light because of whitewashed walls. Apparently he lived alone and liked it. There were bright curtains, freshly laundered, a comfortable chair that tilted back, with a good reading light, and shelves of books. Mike, a compulsive reader, looked at them in some surprise. Erasmus, Montaigne, *Tristram Shandy,* a well-worn *Tom Jones, The Oxford Book of English Verse.*

The superintendent, who said his name was Wilson, bustled around preparing the rum punch. Like many people who live alone, even when they like it, he had stored up a spate of words to pour out on the first captive audience. He had retired on a small pension and social security, he said, after forty years as a bookkeeper, and he had taken this job because it provided him with a comfortable room and enough money for meals and sundries, leaving his pension for small pleasures, books and—

"And rum punch," Mike said with a smile as he accepted the napkin-wrapped glass. For a few minutes the two men sipped the pungent drink, and Mike could feel its warmth dispelling the chill of the night. With a man like this he changed his mind about offering any fancy stories. He'd stick to the truth.

"What do you want to know about Snodgrass?" the superintendent asked abruptly. "I hope the poor devil isn't in any more trouble. He's had about all he can take."

"I'd like to know what's happened to him," Mike said. Seeing the other man's expression he added hastily, "If you are afraid I intend to make him any trouble, you can set your mind at rest, but there are reasons why it is important to find him. Nothing personal. I've never set eyes on the man in my life. What do you know about him?"

The superintendent took a cautious sip of the steaming drink and said that the Snodgrass family—Snodgrass himself, his wife, and two children—had moved into the house at the same time he did, five years before. Snodgrass was a shoe-repair man who had a small but steady business. Every now and then his wife would go away for a while. The superintendent had thought she was visiting her family; then it turned out she was a mental case who had to be institutionalized periodically. Last time, about a year ago, she got so bad he couldn't leave her alone because she wasn't safe any more. She would have violent attacks, destroy furniture, and even, if she fancied she was being ill-treated, strike her children, though fortunately they were both old enough and big enough, especially the son who was in his late twenties, to handle her.

"Anyhow, poor Snodgrass had her committed, and now he goes to see her every Sunday and comes back looking like the wrath of God. Depleted. A broken man."

The superintendent looked at Mike's empty glass and got up to reheat the punch, stirring it so the fragrance of rum and lemons and cinnamon sticks filled the air. He refilled the glass and watched Mike wrap the napkin around it.

"Well," he said when his guest's drink had been sampled and approved of, "the two young ones were as nice as anyone you'd want to meet, well-behaved, attractive, good manners. None of this hippie stuff, long hair and dirty feet and rough ways. The girl wanted to be a singer and you could hear her practicing scales and singing all day long. Sometimes the neighbors would complain, but as they kept their television sets tuned on high, I didn't try to stop her. You have to give a little and take a little."

"Was she good?" Mike asked.

The superintendent shrugged. "I'm tone deaf. But one of our tenants who was a professional musician had great faith in her. Used to talk to her by the hour to encourage her.

"What happened at last was that the girl had a severe disappointment. She believed that some wealthy woman was going to make her an opera star and then changed her mind in favor of someone else. Poor Louisa took a mess of sleeping pills—her father told me later she had a quart bottle full of them that she had been collecting from black-market drugstores for months—and died of it." The superintendent's intelligent eyes rested on Mike's face. "You knew all this."

Mike nodded.

"Poor Snodgrass seemed to age overnight and he began to keep a sharp eye on his son for fear he would go the same way, though I never saw an indication of anything wrong. And then damned if the son didn't disappear. Not a word. Just up and went away, taking with him his father's savings, seven or eight hundred dollars. Mr. Snodgrass hung on here for a while, hoping he would turn up, but I guess he lost hope. He decided it was no use. He gave up the apartment, but whether he went to look for his son or what he had in mind I don't know. He was terribly upset."

"Was he afraid his son would kill himself the way his daughter did?"

"Himself or someone else," the superintendent said. "He talked to me the day he left. He said all three had these sudden attacks of violence. He never could guess what would set them off."

"And he didn't give you a hint as to where he was going?"

"No, I haven't the faintest idea. Does it matter?"

"I'd give a year's pay to know where the son is. If he's in a vengeful frame of mind, he might be intensely dangerous. If you get any word of the father let me know, will you?" He gave the superintendent his card. Then he remembered and gave him the address of Ma Baccante's boardinghouse and the telephone number. "But if you get in touch with me there be discreet, will you? No names. No message except to ask me to call."

The superintendent took the card with its scrawled address and set it carefully on the edge of the bookcase. Mike thanked him for the rum punch. "You're a remarkable man," he said as they shook hands.

The superintendent was amused. "Because I didn't ask questions? You have no conception of the amount of restraint I used. I won't sleep tonight, wondering what this is all about."

Mike laughed and said, "Someday I'll come back and tell you."

"I hope you will. It will be something to look forward to."

"And next time," Mike promised him, touched by

that unconscious betrayal of loneliness, "the drinks will be on me."

He went back to Third Avenue where he looked for a drugstore and went to the telephone booths in the back, fumbling in his pocket for change.

Leonard Field answered sleepily, but he was wide awake when Mike had told him that young Snodgrass had disappeared without a trace. "His father probably alerted the Missing Persons Bureau at the time, but your man, Lieutenant Baxter, would probably want to know, because this thing may tie in with the Conway murder. If young Snodgrass blamed Mrs. Conway for his sister's suicide and if he shared his sister's belief that Miss Evans was responsible for her failure to get Mrs. Conway's support, he could be very bad medicine."

"I'll get a message to the lieutenant at once," Field said grimly. "You're sure the Evans girl is all right?"

"Temporarily. I have a room on the same floor, but I can't be there all the time. And that reminds me, can you give me her home address? I want to look into her background. That comment about 'it's the future that counts' sticks in my mind."

"You'll be careful?"

"I'll be careful," Mike promised him somewhat impatiently, "but we have a potential murderer on the loose, Lenny."

"I can't see what the murderer has to do with Bridget Evans's background."

"Probably nothing at all, but she's—"

"Holding something back. Feeling guilty. You said that before."

"So I did, but there's something more. She's—suspicious. It's almost," Mike groped, "as though she assumed people would be suspicious of her. Expected them to be. I want to know why."

"Well, I never thought you and Sergeant Carmichael would have anything in common. That's the way she impressed him."

Mike wrote down the address. "Do you happen to know who her former employer was?" Field didn't.

The elevator operator at Ma Baccante's was not one of the Baccante brothers but he looked vaguely familiar. "Hi," he said breezily, "didja hear Saul's recital?"

Mike shook his head. The operator grinned. "I guess you don't remember meeting all of us at supper. I'm Heinrich Glotz, fiddle. I have the room next to yours, and Ma gives me my meals for doing night elevator shift as a relief man." He opened the door. "Good night, Mike."

"Good night, Heinrich." Mike walked softly down the uncarpeted hallway with its single light bulb. Most of the rooms were dark. Only two showed lights under them. From one came a girl's soft, provocative laugh and a protest that was not meant to be taken seriously, and Mike's brows went up in an amused arc. From the other lighted room came a blurred voice and then a lower pitched one, quiet, soothing. Peg Reston was looking after Bridget Evans. For this night, at least, she was safe.

6

Mike had not been prepared for the amount of noise that a number of earnest music students can make when they are practicing. Promptly at eight o'clock he was almost lifted out of bed by the sheer volume of the worst outburst of cacophonous sound he had ever experienced. On one side of him a violin, presumably that of the erstwhile elevator operator, was being tuned. From the room he knew to be Saul's, there was the Chopin Revolutionary Étude played at an incredibly slow pace. From a third room came a baritone voice and from a fourth, a cello. How in the name of God, he wondered—and it surprised him that this should be his first thought of the day—did a girl as sick as Bridget Evans endure the noise?

This morning Giuseppi was again on the elevator, and he greeted Mike as an old friend. "Did you hear Saul's recital?"

Mike shook his head.

"Too bad. It was terrific. He's got it made, I'm telling you. You're late this morning." His manner was severe.

"Too late for breakfast?" Mike asked hopefully, as he had not been impressed by Ma Baccante's cooking.

"Oh, no. Go on down. She's still serving. At least the

food hasn't been put away yet. But mostly the kids like to get started early, you know."

Leaving the top floor with its resident students practicing provided no escape from the noise. On floor after floor Mike was bombarded by voices, pianos, strings, wind instruments, interspersed by the comments of teachers.

Ma Baccante was alone in the basement dining room except for Peg Reston whose red hair was brushed back neatly in a pony tail that was no longer fashionable but that somehow suited her. She had apparently finished her breakfast, and now she was enjoying a chat with Ma. Before her on a small plate was a glass of milk.

"No," she was saying in her warm voice as Mike walked in, "this is all she can take now. Perhaps some clear soup later." She looked up to smile. "Good morning."

"Good morning, Mike," Ma said. "What'll it be: scrambled eggs or pancakes?"

"Eggs. And can I have them fried?"

"Of course. Sunny-side up?" She bustled out of the room, and Mike asked, "How's your patient?"

"Not doing too well." Peg shook her head. "But the doctor warned me there wouldn't be much change for at least twenty-four hours. Her fever is still high and she's—not delirious exactly but not clear in her head. She sleeps a lot, of course, but at least she's no worse."

"You are being extremely kind to a stranger."

She smiled. "Well, you can't pass by on the other side."

"It's been known to happen."

Her eyes were shadowed. "Yes, it's been known to happen, but people like that belong outside the human race."

"Are you going to get some rest?"

She was surprised. "Oh, I'm all right. Actually, I slept most of the night. She didn't need much. And Ma is having a cot moved into her room today so I'll be as snug as in my own room." As Ma came in with a cup of coffee for Mike, Peg nodded to them both, took the glass of milk, and went to ring for the elevator.

"That's a nice girl," Ma said. "A mighty nice girl. I'd like to see my boys marry girls as nice as that one. Too bad she isn't prettier. Good looks may not last but they're molasses for catching men in the first place. I meant to ask you what's your instrument? If it's piano there's no place for one in your room, of course, but there's an upright on the fourth floor you can rent to practice on from one to four every day and there's a baby grand you might get from eight to eleven on the first floor. Miss Murchison has her studio there but she teaches uptown mornings. And if Saul leaves—you heard his recital?"

"How was it?"

Ma kissed her fingers. *"Bellissima.* Rave notices this morning. My students were wild when they got home. And such a program too: the Waldstein and the Schumann Fantasia and so many Chopin études. I thought it was too much, putting all his wares in the store window, as you might say, but it paid off in spades. You'd never guess who came around to see him after he finished last night—a representative from the Hurok office. Mrs. Conway had dropped them a hint that Saul was worth watching. So at least one of my students is going to be famous. You watch and see. And maybe another: that is, if Bridget hasn't ruined her voice, talking and all when her throat was in that shape."

"Good, is she?"

71

"You should hear her range, larger than Sills, a light voice, of course, but not cold like most coloraturas, a lot of warmth in it, and something about her—she'll have the stage presence of a Callas. God, I get to talking and forget your breakfast. That's what my boys are always saying to me. 'Ma,' they say, 'if you'd just stop talking and get busy.' "

When she reappeared with a plate of toast and eggs, Frank Saunders came into the dining room and pulled out a chair, nodding to Mike. Ma, who had responded as most women did to Mike's casual charm, was severe. "You're late. I can't serve breakfast all morning."

"That's all right," he assured her. "I'll go out and pick up something." He rubbed his head. "I didn't sleep much."

"I'll bring you some coffee," Ma relented. "You're not coming down with anything, are you?"

"I kept hearing Bridget cough and it worried me. Shouldn't we get another doctor?"

Ma patted his shoulder. "She'll be all right and she's in good hands. You can't neglect your own work, you know."

"What is your field?" Mike asked.

"I'm a composer. Right now I'm working on an opera."

"Have you done the book yourself?" Mike was interested. This was something, at least, that he knew about.

Frank nodded. "I think I've got something worth doing. It's experimental, of course, and it's timely. Relevant. And I've worked out a novel and dramatic way of treating it. I call it *The Broken Link*. It's about the generation gap, with part of the music conventional and part of it mod—the two generations. It dramatizes the clash. I've got a terrific role for a coloratura." He met Mike's ironic eyes and flushed. "Are you planning to stay here long?" he asked, trying awkwardly to shift the conversation away from himself and his work.

"I have no plans."

"Now where do you want to start practicing, Mike?" Ma asked him. "You can use the fourth floor room this afternoon, and I'll see Miss Murchison when she comes in." Apparently she had assumed that Mike played the piano.

"We'll let it go for a day or so. This morning I have to go out on business. Don't expect me for lunch."

"Out on a day like this?" She shook her head. "Well, you wrap up good. Mind now."

II

Mike shook hands with Lieutenant Baxter and with Sergeant Carmichael and looked around him with frank curiosity. "This is the first time I've been in a police station."

"And the first time you've tried your hand at police work?" Baxter asked politely.

Mike grinned at him disarmingly. "I hope Mr. Field didn't give you that impression. It was his idea that I take a look at Miss Evans—"

"What's your impression of her?"

Mike explained that he had moved into the building where she lived so that he could be in a position to keep an eye on her. He had got an extra break because the music students who lived there ate their meals at Ma Baccante's table. At the moment she was seriously ill and being looked after by one of the music students who appeared to be a competent young woman.

"You've got to watch Evans," Carmichael warned him. "That girl's a congenital liar. That stuff she handed me about the large, young man—"

"I believe in the large, young man," Mike said quietly.

Baxter, looking from one man to the other, made no comment. After a moment's hesitation, Mike let the matter drop. Instead he described his interview with the superintendent at the building where the missing Snodgrass had lived. Baxter nodded. Mr. Field had told him about the missing Snodgrass and his son and that they were being hunted. Farfetched to assume that the son would share his sister's delusions and try to avenge her, though it was always possible. In police work anything was possible.

"There's one thing," Mike said hesitantly. "The superintendent in the building where Snodgrass lived with his family said there was another tenant there who was greatly impressed by Louisa's voice, a professional musician of some sort. It might be worth while checking with him."

"Why?" Baxter asked in amusement.

"To find out how justified the girl's disappointment might have been."

Baxter dismissed the idea with a slight gesture. "I set up this appointment to ask just what you have in mind, Mr. Graves."

"I'm going up to that Connecticut town from which Miss Evans came to see what I can find out about her background."

"That can't do any harm. Let me know what you pick up."

"If anything," Mike said.

"If anything, of course. And I'd better give you something in the way of identification in case people clam up." The lieutenant scrawled a few words on an official card. "Good luck to you."

III

Mike eased his Chrysler out of the garage and headed slowly toward Riverside Drive and the Henry Hudson Parkway, trying to avoid spraying slush on passersby, the windshield wipers moving smoothly, clearing off snow, the heater gradually taking the chill out of the air.

The Parkway was almost deserted because of the treacherous road conditions. Although he was a careful driver, Mike risked an occasional glance to right and left. On the left was the Hudson, presumably flowing in its usual fashion under its thick coating of ice. Ahead was the span of the George Washington Bridge, seen dimly through a curtain of snow. Occasionally on a side street, he made out the top of a parked car now snowbound or heard the grinding of a truck trying to get up an icy street.

He was, he told himself, probably on a wild-goose chase, in search of the background of the girl whom Sergeant Carmichael so deeply distrusted. What he should be doing, at least what someone should be doing, was hunting for the missing Snodgrass, but this the police could do far better than he. Probably they would try to reach the father, and they could get some leads in that way.

The chances were a hundred to one, he told himself without believing a word of it, that Snodgrass had no designs on Bridget Evans. Just because his sister had blamed her—it didn't make sense that he would share her aberration. But, Mike reminded himself, he wasn't dealing with sense, not with a rational person, just a person who, most alarmingly, gave the impression of being rational, perfectly normal. It was not a pleasant feeling. And Bridget was in no shape to defend herself. But she didn't need to defend herself, he argued. She had Peg Reston, a most dependable person. She had her adoring watchdog, Frank Saunders. For the time being that was just as well. What he meant by "the time being" Mike did not analyze to himself.

The New England village in which Bridget Evans had grown up was, at least around the green, a typically picturesque village, with its stately, widely spaced colonial houses, elms and maples scattered over the grounds, the slim white spire of a church. The side streets were less attractive, grubby and shabby, old houses turned into rooming houses or into shops.

Whatever the financial circumstances of Bridget Evans's father, he had lived in the best part of town. The number Leonard Field had supplied was at the top of the green, looking down at its snowy expanse, a spacious colonial house with the paint fresh and white and everything in beautiful condition. Somehow Mike had not expected Bridget to come from a background like this. No one who lived in that house, maintained as it was, should need help to pay for music lessons. The place looked like an illustration for a sentimental Christmas story. All it lacked was a sleigh drawn up before the entrance and a couple of horses with bells on their harnesses.

Mike lifted the polished knocker and heard the sound echo in the house, heard heavy deliberate steps. The woman who opened the door was about fifty and overweight. On her plump face was a fixed smile like that on the face of a dolphin, but considerably less engaging, and she had the coldest eyes Mike had ever encountered. As he was a man of more than average attractions, he was not often rebuffed by women; so he was not prepared for her "Well?" uttered in an unencouraging tone. "I'm not buying anything."

"I'm not selling anything. Are you Mrs. Evans?"

"No, I'm Mrs. Hillard."

"But the Evanses do live here?"

"Mr. Evans died over a year ago. The house belongs to me now."

"Oh?"

"I was the housekeeper for twenty-five years. Not that it concerns you."

"Well, it might in a way. I'm from the New York police, Mrs.—uh—"

"Hillard. Do you have any credentials?"

Blessing Baxter for his foresight, Mike was able to satisfy her, and she said ungraciously, that meaningless smile plastered on her face, "You can come in if you like."

How in the name of heaven, Mike wondered, had any man been able to endure this woman for twenty-five years? And if she was the one who had had the care of Bridget, God help the girl!

The room into which she took him was unexpectedly beautiful. Mike recognized the wallpaper as a famous French design; the woodwork was shining; there were fine rugs scattered over the treacherously waxed, wide floor boards. Inexperienced as he was in the field it was apparent even to his untutored eyes that the room must contain a fortune in antiques. The furniture smelled of lemon oil and was in mint condition. The whole room belonged in a museum, beautiful and dead. It was so unlived in that it seemed airless. The housekeeper probably polished it every day and then sat in a crowded room with an old-fashioned rocking chair and a Tiffany lamp.

"The reason I came," he began as soon as she was seated, "was—"

"I can guess," Mrs. Hillard interrupted. "It's about Bridget. I suppose she's in some kind of trouble."

"Why do you assume that?"

There was something unnerving about the woman's incessant smile that never warmed the cold eyes. "Because she always was. Bad blood there and it showed from the beginning. I ought to know. I guess I know her better than anyone in the world except for her father."

"What was he like?" Mike asked.

Her face brightened. "He was a good man, a good provider, a regular churchgoer. A man who upheld all the good causes and fought the bad tendencies. He was a serious man, never anything frivolous about him, nothing foolish—except when he got married. There are some women who can make a fool out of the most sensible men. She was eighteen and he was thirty-eight but he fell in love with her. His mother didn't like it much, I can tell you that. He was a good man and she figured that he had settled down and he would never marry. I'd been housekeeper for his mother for a couple of years when he met the girl. He'd gone on vacation to the shore. First time he'd ever gone without his mother. I can still remember how she kept saying, 'I never should have let him go alone.' "

"Do you mind if I smoke?" Mike asked.

"No one has ever smoked in this house, young man." When Mike had returned his cigarette pack to his pocket, she went on, "Well, it just about killed her. She took to her bed and she never got up again. I guess Mr. Evans blamed himself. Anyhow, it was too late to mend matters. He had brought his bride home, a little thing, all eyes, a lot like Bridget. I could see from the beginning that the marriage wouldn't work. At first she was always dancing and singing and trying to coax Mr. Evans to go out to the movies or to dinner or I don't know what."

Mike's bland expression revealed nothing of his thoughts. Even if she could have read them, however, it is unlikely they would have had any effect on her deep complacency and the bitter resentment, which she took for outraged virtue, against a younger and prettier woman.

"Well, after while she seemed to settle down. She didn't keep nagging him to do things but she didn't sing much, though she had a real pretty voice. And then the baby came. It must have been two years later that it happened. One afternoon while I was giving old Mrs. Evans her daily massage, young Mrs. Evans just slipped out of the house, taking the little girl and leaving a note that said, 'No one can live without any love or kindness. I am going to marry Sam Lewis as soon as I am free.'

"Well, Mrs. Evans, bedridden or not, was still mistress of this house, and she said, 'I told you so,' and Mr. Evans got a divorce and custody of Bridget, because he didn't think she should be brought up by an immoral mother. He brought her back here and said, 'Mrs. Hillard, I am going to put my daughter in your hands. You'll have her to raise so she won't turn out like her mother.'

"I did my best for her but I had my hands full, I can tell you that. Why she wasn't five before I discovered that she was a liar. One day she was out playing and came in with a kitten. She swore it had followed her home, which was a barefaced lie because I had seen her coaxing it along. When I said she had to put it out, she cried and carried on and said she didn't have anything, no mother, no friends, no pets. Well, from then on her father and I watched her pretty close, I can tell you. We never knew when she would be telling the truth. Once a liar always a liar is what I say."

Automatically Mike reached for his cigarettes and his lighter and caught her eye. His hand dropped to his side. The poor little devil! She had done nothing to deserve this treatment. Whatever she might have done later—he broke off. That way of thinking was unprofitable.

"Well, when she started growing up she looked more and more like her mother, so I kept a strict watch. I don't need to tell you that. She had to come straight home from school every day. And then the music teacher at school told her she had a beautiful voice and she should have it trained. After that we never had any peace. She went around singing half the time. Even when her father put his foot down and said no child of his was to go posturing and displaying herself on the stage, her teacher, an interfering old fool, had the nerve to come here and try to convince him that he had no right—her own father!—to prevent her from having a brilliant career as an opera singer and wasting an exceptionally lovely voice. A gift from God, he called it." She sniffed and, for the first time, laughed.

"Who was this teacher?"

"Jonathan Davis. He still teaches music around here in the public schools. Well, Mr. Evans had a heart attack and he decided to put his house in order, as the saying goes. He told me he was going to leave me this house and what else he had as a token of gratitude for the years I had devoted so selflessly to his daughter. A very pretty thought. He left her nothing but a small insurance policy because he couldn't trust her with much money."

And you made sure he couldn't, Mike thought. You

fanned his distrust. You practically kept the girl a prisoner. I wonder whether you were aiming to become the second Mrs. Evans or whether you were satisfied to collar the works.

The meaningless smile deepened. "What has Bridget done now? I saw by the paper she'd found some rich woman to pay for her singing lessons and leave her a fortune, and then the woman died." There was a world of innuendo in her voice.

Mike glanced at his watch, gave an exclamation of concern, and got out before she could ask another question and gratefully drew in a long breath of clean air when he reached the sidewalk.

IV

Jonathan Davis was alone in a small soundproof room, listening critically to a recording of some French folk songs when Mike found him. He was a slight man of sixty who looked up inquiringly when Mike came in. The latter explained that he had been checking on the background of Bridget Evans.

"And you got my name from Mrs. Hillard? Don't tell me what she said about me. She is, without exception, the most unpleasant woman I ever encountered. I hope Bridget is all right."

"Tell me what you know about her."

Davis looked him over thoughtfully before he made up his mind. "All right, I don't mind telling you what I know, because there isn't a single thing that could do her a scrap of harm. So if you are looking for scandal or gossip, you are wasting your time." As Mike did not move Davis leaned back in his chair, summoning up his memories of Bridget Evans.

She had been, he said, a loving child with no one to

love, a laughing child who never heard laughter, a friendly child who had no friends. She couldn't ask anyone to the house or go to parties. She became withdrawn and distrustful because she had never been trusted. She blamed herself for things of which she was guiltless. And that, if anyone wanted to know, was the work of the housekeeper.

"I suppose you know about her mother," Davis said.

"At least the Hillard version."

"You should have seen her when she was first married. Like sunlight. But Evans and his cannibal mother and that damned housekeeper among them broke her spirit. How she ever got up the courage to run away, unless it was sheer desperation, I'll never know, but I hope to God she had better luck with her second marriage. Evans took Bridget, you know. He claimed it was to save her from her mother's influence; actually he wanted to punish the poor girl.

"I discovered that Bridget had a phenomenal voice, and I wanted her to have better training than I am equipped to give her. I know my limitations. I can teach children to read music and to sing a bit and can give them a smattering of music appreciation—or at least introduce them to great music and try to help them hear what it has to say—but I'm not competent to work with a voice like Bridget's. Bad training could destroy it. Anyhow, her father categorically refused to let her sing. To him music meant theater and theater meant vice."

When the old man died, Davis urged the girl to take the pittance her father left her and go to New York. "You know the Hillard woman got practically everything?" When Mike nodded, Davis went on. He knew of Madame Woolf's reputation as a teacher and arranged to have her hear Bridget sing. Then when she was enthusiastic, Bridget got a job to pay for her singing lessons. She wrote several times to tell Davis how she was getting along with her lessons and to say she had a part-time job.

Did he, Mike broke in to ask, happen to know the name of her employer?

This time Davis was not so prompt to reply. He hesitated a bit before he said, rather reluctantly, "A Mrs. Gordon Briggs, somewhere on Central Park West in New York. Well, Bridget wrote that she had lost her job and that she would have to give up singing lessons. The last letter I had from her said that Madame Woolf had asked Mrs. Elizabeth Conway, the music patron, to hear her, and the latter had been excited about her voice.

"I think," Davis said, polishing his glasses, "she was happier than she had ever been in her life. And now I understand from the radio that the poor girl found Mrs. Conway's dead body. I hope to God nothing has happened to her. She has had so little out of life. So very little!"

V

The wheels spun on frozen snow and then caught. Mike eased the car onto the road and switched on the heater. The snow-covered green with its white houses was like a postcard view of New England prettiness but, recalling the atmosphere of the Evans house, Mike felt that the truth might be somewhat closer to O'Neill.

While he negotiated the Saw Mill River Parkway, slowed by a snowplow ahead, he sorted out the contrasting pictures of Bridget Evans he had received. An untrustworthy liar who had inherited bad blood; the victim of a father who, whether he knew it or not, used her as a whipping boy to revenge himself on her mother; and of that smiling jailor of a housekeeper who had made sure that no one would trust her. No wonder the girl was on the defensive, if that was true. If that was true, he reminded himself cautiously.

Mrs. Gordon Briggs, as he learned from a telephone directory, lived in a big apartment building on Central Park West, only two blocks from his mother's apartment. He garaged his car and called his mother to say he would be home for lunch. Perhaps one-thirty.

The man at the switchboard regretted that Mrs. Briggs was unacquainted with Mr. Graves and could not see him.

"Tell her I am here with credentials from the homicide division of the New York police force." Mike believed in bringing out the big guns when they would save time.

The switchboard operator murmured inaudibly in the telephone and then said, "Yes, sir. The elevator on your right, sir. Eighth floor."

A uniformed maid admitted him and took him into a huge drawing room with a spectacular view of Central Park and Fifth Avenue, the walls covered with somber paintings that appeared to be the work of minor artists imitating the seventeenth-century Dutch school.

Mrs. Briggs came into the room, a small dominant woman with gray hair exquisitely dressed, a simple black dress with a necklace of matched pearls, a sharp nose with a pink tip, and an arrogant manner that, in a man, would have been bluster. She might have been more impressive if she had not been frightened. The fear was in the flicker of her eyelids, the tension of her lips, the restless hands.

"Yes, Mr.—" She did not ask him to sit down.

"Graves. Michael Graves." What was she afraid of?

Not the police in the sense that ignorant people feared them. Then there must be a specific reason, for the usual ones would not apply in this atmosphere of assured wealth and stability.

"You once employed a Miss Bridget Evans as a secretary, didn't you?"

Her eyelids flickered again. Mrs. Briggs went to close the door. "Sit down, Mr. Graves, but I hope you won't take long. Ten minutes—"

She sure as hell wants to get rid of me, Mike thought. What gives? Aloud he said, "Ten minutes should be ample. You did hire Miss Evans?"

"Yes." She wasn't going to volunteer any information.

"And then you dismissed her without a recommendation. Why was that?"

"I don't understand why you are asking me these questions."

Mike did not explain; he waited, watching the restless, betraying hands. For months he had been pointing out to the actors in his television plays that hands were more revealing than faces. As he expected, Mrs. Briggs found his silence unnerving.

"Unfortunately," he felt that she was groping for words, "Miss Evans proved to be untrustworthy."

"In what way?"

"I had hoped we might forget the whole unpleasant episode." When Mike gave her no help, she said reluctantly, "I missed pieces of jewelry on several occasions. At first I naturally assumed that I had mislaid them. Then a valuable diamond bracelet disappeared, and I sent for the police. In a pillow slip in Miss Evans's room the policeman found my bracelet. She denied taking it, but her manner was—hostile and on the defensive. No one believed her, of course."

"You had her arrested?"

"No, as it happened my son came home while the policeman was there. He is very young and impressionable, and Miss Evans is a pretty girl. He urged me, as long as I had recovered the bracelet, to drop the charge. He thought it would be unfortunate for a girl planning a public career, as we understood she was, to have a police record, so I agreed."

"And then?"

She raised her brows. "That's all. Miss Evans left here at once, of course." Mrs. Briggs stood up. "I know nothing more about the girl except what I have read in the papers—that she has been involved in the murder of that Mrs. Conway who left her a substantial legacy."

A poisonous woman, Mike thought, but, on the stand, a dangerous foe, with her impregnable social position and her poise. He thanked her and saw that the tension had gone, that her hands had relaxed. What had she been afraid of? Just as she opened the door to the foyer, the outer door opened and a young man came in and handed his hat and overcoat to the maid who had hurried into the foyer. He glanced at Mike in surprise. Mrs. Briggs caught her breath. Mike had the strongest impression that she conquered an impulse to close the drawing room door, shutting him away from the foyer and the young man. Then she said, "Good afternoon," in a chilly tone of dismissal, and Mike felt that she was pushing him by an effort of will toward the outer door.

He played a hunch. "Is this your son?"

"Good afternoon," she repeated.

The young man who had started up a flight of stairs, paused, turned back. "I am Chester Briggs. You are—"

"Michael Graves."

"That name's familiar. Theater, isn't it?"

Mike said hastily, "Police. Homicide division."

"You are keeping Mr. Graves waiting, dear."

"I am in no hurry," Mike told her. "I'd like a word with you, Mr. Briggs, if you don't mind answering a question."

"This is quite absurd," Mrs. Briggs said sharply.

"What about?" Chester asked.

"Miss Bridget Evans."

"Chester!"

He put his hand on his mother's arm, turned her toward the stairs, and nodded his head toward the big drawing room. "Come in, Mr. Graves."

With a small despairing gesture, Mrs. Briggs started up the stairs to the second floor of the duplex, without a backward look. Chester waved Mike to a chair, pushed forward a box of cigarettes and indicated a lighter. When they had lighted up, he asked, "What can I tell you about Bridget Evans?" He was facing the light, not a bad-looking fellow, Mike thought appraisingly. A good forehead and nose but a weak mouth and chin. Not a happy face. Some sort of conflict there.

"It's a simple question, Mr. Briggs. In your opinion is Bridget Evans truthful or is she a liar?"

The boy tapped his cigarette, and Mike noticed the slight tremor in his fingers. "Why do you want to know?"

"Here it is, Mr. Briggs. Miss Evans claims that she saw Mrs. Conway's murderer. You have read about the Conway case? Good. Now the point is this: if she lied about that man she may be the killer herself or protecting someone else. If she told the truth she could be in considerable danger from the man she described and whom she can identify. Clear?"

"Quite clear. And you came here because you heard of the theft of my mother's bracelet, and she told you Bridget is a thief and a liar. Correct?"

Mike nodded. My God, he thought, I've struck pay dirt!

Chester pressed out his cigarette with an air of decision. He was very white, almost as though he was about to be sick. "This is the story of what really happened. I got hooked on heroin. Hooked but good. It took more cash than I could raise without making some highly unpleasant explanations to my mother. So I stole a couple of pieces of her jewelry, a ring and some earrings she never wore, and hocked them. Then I took her diamond bracelet. Before I could dispose of it, she missed it and suspected Bridget, who was the only new employee, and called the police. It was too late then to call off the police; because one was already in the house questioning Bridget; so I got my mother out of the room and told her the truth.

"Well, she's a proud woman, and I'm her only child and she wouldn't let me take the blame. So we compromised. I gave her the bracelet and she hid it in Bridget's room where the cop could find it. I—went along on it because she promised to get Bridget off the hook. The cop could see something was up; I imagine he thought I was having an affair with her and that was why I was trying to get her off."

"Were you?" Mike was surprised to discover how casual his tone was.

Chester laughed a little. "No such luck. Anyhow that's not what I wanted. I'd have married her like a shot if she'd seen it that way. Well, my mother had to withdraw the charge and she let Bridget go and I've been taking the cure. It's hell, of course, but it seems to be working. I suppose you think I'm a bastard."

"That doesn't concern me. The point is not how you and your mother have victimized the girl, the point is whether or not she is a liar."

"She isn't. She's completely trustworthy. I can't seem to forget the way she stood there hoping the cop would believe her and seeing that he didn't."

"Thank you, Mr. Briggs."

"I guess this explanation is long overdue. I'm sorry. I'm really sorry."

"Save it for Miss Evans."

7

On the third morning Bridget awakened to look around her with clear eyes and the knowledge that her skin felt cool and her fever was gone. She heard the endless tumult of practicing. The world had come back to normal, as normal as it could ever be again without Liz. Liz with her deep understanding and her astringent approach to problems that was more bracing than all the sentimental goodwill in the world.

A tap on the door was followed by the red-headed girl who was carrying a tray. "Oh, good! You look much better this morning."

"I feel fine," Bridget said, "and I'm starving."

"That will please Ma." Peg settled the tray on Bridget's knees and propped another pillow behind her. She did things with a minimum of fuss. "You aren't to speak a word until you have eaten everything. Ma's orders." She pulled a chair near the bed and sat down, her hands loosely clasped on her lap. A restful person.

"No one could possibly have been kinder," Bridget said. "I can't thank you for all you've done."

"I've had a lot of experience nursing and it was that or go to the hospital."

"How long have I been ill?"

"Just three days."

"And I didn't even go to Liz's funeral."

"You mean Mrs. Conway? She left instructions that she did not want any funeral services, but there was a memorial service yesterday. Crowded. Everyone you ever heard of in the field of music and some who had even flown in from the West Coast and Europe. And tributes from the directors of the Met and Covent Garden and La Scala. People really seemed to love her."

"People did love her. Don't make any mistake about that. Why did you go? Curiosity?"

There was an odd expression on Peg's face. "In a way you might call it that."

"I'm sorry." Bridget was contrite. "You have been incredibly kind to a total stranger, and then I was rude to you. I'm just—touchy where Liz is concerned."

Peg brushed aside the apology. "We aren't strangers now, I hope. I've been away so long I don't know anyone in New York except my teacher, and he's left for Baltimore where his son has to have a dangerous operation; so I'm at loose ends. I could use a friend."

"So could I. Without Liz—" Bridget pushed away her tray. "I'll have to get up."

"You're as weak as a cat."

"But I haven't practiced for a week and I've missed two lessons and Madame Woolf will be furious."

Peg did not argue. She sat relaxed and quiet while Bridget swung her feet onto the floor and then clutched at the bed to steady herself until the dizziness disappeared and her legs stopped tingling. She got up slowly and walked to the window and back to a chair into which she subsided, panting, a fine moisture on her forehead and upper lip.

"And the moral of that is," Peg murmured.

"Yes, I see what you mean." When Peg had helped her back into bed Bridget asked, "What's been going on?"

Peg grinned. "Those flowers are from Frank Saunders, if you need to be told. You seem to have made quite an impact. Whenever I go out of this room, he's waiting to ask about you. In fact, you are practically all he talks about."

Bridget smiled. "Except his opera."

"Except his opera," Peg agreed. "He is certainly pregnant with opera. I hope it will be a successful delivery, but I do get a little tired of hearing about relevance."

Bridget laughed. "Just the same, he is nice, isn't he?"

"Very nice and very devoted. I hope you reciprocate. Devoted men are not to be sneezed at."

"I wouldn't dream of sneezing. He's the only one who ever believed in me, except for Liz, of course."

Peg's eyes were intent. "But the police believed you when you described that murderer."

"I'm not so sure they did. Not sure at all."

"But you were sure enough of yourself to describe him as a murderer."

"Yes. Oh, let's forget it for now! What about Saul?"

"He's been offered a fine contract; the big mogul himself is taking him on."

"Liz would have been so pleased! She had faith in him right from the very beginning."

Peg picked up the breakfast tray. "What do I tell Frank?"

"Thank him for the flowers—and all his kindness. I'll be down to dinner tonight."

But it was the following night before Bridget was able to make her first appearance at the table in the basement. In honor of the occasion, for everything was an excuse for a celebration with Ma, she arranged a buffet, and Frank provided some bottles of Chianti. Bridget looked at herself in the mirror before going downstairs. She had lost a lot of weight and there were hollows under her cheekbones, hollows at her temples, hollows at her wrists. Her eyes looked too big for her face.

She was moving lethargically when she took the elevator to the basement, but she was welcomed with so much eagerness and such warmth and so gay a festive spirit that she shook off her apathy. Frank hovered solicitously, his face alight, eager to wait on her and apparently determined to give her half the food from the buffet.

Mike Graves had been accepted as part of the family by everyone except Frank, who maintained a watchful attitude. When Frank had filled her plate, Mike brought her a glass of wine.

"Welcome home," he said, raising his glass and smiling at her. It was a nice smile and she found herself smiling back.

"And this time you stay put," Frank declared.

Peg looked at the girl hedged in by the two young men and settled herself beside Saul, a relaxed and self-confident Saul since his successful debut. The rest of the students were exhilarated by Saul's success. What had happened to him could happen to them. They drank to his future and to Bridget's restoration to health and to the newcomers. Bridget was not aware of the effect of the unaccustomed wine after a debilitating illness until she was shocked to hear herself give a high-pitched giggle. The room seemed to be stiflingly hot, the faces around her were blurred, the conversation was difficult to follow.

"She can't possibly be drunk," Peg said. "Not on that amount of Chianti. A child could drink that much without harm. What on earth is wrong with her?"

"Have you been noticing anything wrong?" That was Mike, the attractive newcomer.

"She's been ill," Frank said defensively. "That's all that's the matter."

They were speaking of her, Bridget thought, as though she weren't there.

"Well," Peg said, "I don't understand how pneumonia could have such an effect; I nursed my mother through that, though I suppose people do react differently."

"Bridget is no drinker," Ma declared. "I've known her for nearly a year and she's as pretty behaved a girl as you could find except now and then when she gets into one of her moods."

"Moods?" That was Mike again, casual as though he wasn't particuarly interested.

"Sort of suspicious, as though she didn't trust people or thought they didn't trust her. I can't explain. It's a way she has as if she were saying, 'Well, believe it or not, that's my story.' If people didn't know what a nice girl she really is, it could set them against her. But, drunk or not, she ought to be in bed. She's out on her feet."

"I'll put her to bed," Peg offered, "if someone will give me a hand in taking her back to her room."

"I'll help," Mike said.

"I'll help," Frank echoed.

"I don't need help," Bridget muttered, but the words were blurred; they didn't come out right.

Mike brushed Frank aside, picked Bridget up and, with Frank crowded close behind, carried her to the elevator where Enzo, who wasn't singing that night, clucked in disapproval and concern. Peg opened Bridget's door. "If you'll just put her on—" She broke off, her breath caught in a sharp hiss. After a moment she said, "So that's it. The poor little devil."

Frank looked at the hypodermic on the dressing table and his head jerked with his stunned surprise. "No!"

Mike put Bridget on the bed. "Can you manage her now?"

"Oh, yes, I—*what are you doing?*"

"Removing the evidence." Mike's voice was cool.

"Why?"

"It won't do her any good, will it?"

There was a little pause and then Peg said, "You're the only one who doesn't seem to be surprised, Mike."

"I knew at dinner that the girl wasn't drunk; she was drugged."

And that was the first incident.

II

When she awakened late the next morning with a cottony mouth and a lurking nausea Bridget tried to puzzle out the events of the night before. She had been drugged and Mike had removed a hypodermic from her room. Only how had it got there. And when? And why? And who?

Who? That was the important thing. She must have taken the dope, whatever it was, in the Chianti, as she certainly had not taken it by hypodermic. Someone had deliberately planted the evidence in her room and put some drug in her glass at the table.

She stared at the window and the dim gray light that filtered through. At least it wasn't snowing. She tried to figure out the puzzle. Because she had been ill, everyone at the buffet supper had waited on her—bringing her food and a glass of water and keeping her wine glass filled. Everyone. Most of them she had known for almost a year. Her knowledge of Frank dated from only a few weeks, but, from the beginning, he had been in love with her or wanted her for his leading role in the opera, and she grinned to herself. That left Peg and Mike as the only newcomers, and Peg had waited on her like a mother while she was ill. So— Mike? And it had to be one of the boarders as they were the only ones who lived on the top floor and had access to her room.

The practicing was proceeding exuberantly. Saul was tackling a Prokofiev sonata. How very good he was! A violin was repeating a passage over and over.

Giuseppi slid over the elevator door and this morning he took her down to the basement in disapproving silence. Ma Baccante, Peg, Frank, and Mike were sitting at the table, obviously waiting for her. The two men got up as she came in.

She braced herself. "I don't know just what happened last night but I'm terribly sorry I was a nuisance. I can swear to you that I've never knowingly taken any dope in my life."

How many times before she had stood like this before accusing eyes and had not been believed. She made a little gesture of defeat and pulled out a chair.

"I d—don't believe you t—took d—dope," Frank stuttered in earnestness and embarrassment. "It was just the Chianti, no matter what Mike says."

Ma Baccante brought Bridget a cup of coffee, eying her warily as though not sure of what she might do.

"How do you feel?" Peg broke the awkward silence.

Bridget was aware of Frank's solicitous look, of Mike's measuring look. "Groggy. Maybe I'll do better after I've had some coffee. I don't want to eat because

I have a lesson this morning."

Mike sat with a cup of coffee cooling in front of him, obviously waiting for a chance to speak to Bridget alone, but Peg remained seated until Bridget had finished a bowl of cereal and then accompanied her upstairs. With a shrug Mike went to his own room.

When Peg had followed Bridget into her room she asked, "What do you know about Mike Graves?"

"Nothing. I never saw him until I came back from the hospital. Why?"

"There's something queer about the way he acts. He was watching you all through dinner last night and he's the one who said you were doped and not drunk and he took away the hypodermic. I didn't like that."

"Are you trying to tell me Mike was responsible for what happened to me last night?"

"Well, you got that dope either knowingly or unknowingly. And when you come right down to it, what is Mike Graves doing in this galère? He isn't a music student, and who else would be willing to put up with this racket?"

"Why don't you ask him?"

"Oh, I did." Peg was amused. "He told me a whopper. He said he was a sidewalk artist, one of those people who do lightning portraits for a dollar, and he moved here because it is cheap. Which, my pet, is a thundering lie. His suit didn't cost a penny less than three hundred dollars and his shoes are handmade and his overcoat came from one of the most exclusive tailors in London. His wardrobe cost more than most of us have to live on for a year. So what is he doing at Ma's table?"

"You don't like him, do you?"

"Yes, I do." Peg surprised her by saying. "He's so attractive in that casual, don't-give-a-damn way of his that any woman would like him, and it's a cinch that a lot of them have, but I wouldn't trust him an inch. Whatever he has on his mind, it isn't sidewalk portraits."

"Well, it can't be me." Bridget took a questioning look at herself in the mirror and frowned at what she saw. The pupils of her eyes had narrowed to pinpoints. She slipped on the storm boots Peg had procured for her and put on her heavy coat, pulling the lined hood down over her hair and ears. Even so the knife edge of cold slashed at her cheeks when she went out into the street, made the tip of her nose tingle, and brought water to her eyes.

Madame Woolf's studio was in the Carnegie Hall building, a cavernous room with a skylight. On winter days it was as dark as a cave, with lamps lighting small areas of the gloom. There was a concert grand piano in the middle of the room, a couch and easy chairs, a library of music, and a record player. Madame was short and fat; she had an unfortunate predilection for long black velvet robes and gold slippers with high heels and a preposterous red wig. She looked ridiculous, and she was probably the finest teacher in her field. She could afford to pick and choose her pupils and she did. When they failed to satisfy her expectations, she got rid of them without ceremony, heedless of tears or complaints. A pupil who met her exacting requirements usually was launched on a successful professional career. She was hardworking, painstaking, and completely ruthless. Her pupils were terrified of her and they adored her.

She gave Bridget a sharp look and exclaimed in concern over her loss of weight and her general appearance. The look deepened. "What have you been taking?" She tipped back Bridget's chin, looked at her eyes. "Understand this, *petite*. Drug addiction I will not tolerate. Is that clear?"

Bridget nodded.

"Well, I suppose you've been taking some barbiturate to help you sleep after the shock of finding Liz Conway and practically catching her murderer in the act. She is a terrible loss to the music community and you were close to her, weren't you? She took more pains with you personally than she did with any of the other students she sponsored. You may be worrying about your lessons, but I can assure you she paid me through the spring; so that is taken care of, and you'll probably have your inheritance by then." Madame Woolf did not teach pupils who could not pay; she regarded such procedure as unbusinesslike and foolish sentimentality. When Bridget made no reply she said, "You've been ill?"

"Pneumonia," Bridget explained how it had happened.

"That was foolish of you but it's past. You will not make the same mistake again. Only stupid people repeat the pattern of their mistakes. Now to work. You have lost three lessons and I cannot make them up because the time was set aside for you." Madame seated herself at the piano and flipped open a score. Before Bridget had sung half a dozen phrases, the score was slapped shut. "That's enough. You have been putting too much strain on your voice."

"But—"

"Listen to me. You have a lovely coloratura and an exceptional range. Your technique is sound and it has improved by leaps and bounds. If all had gone well—"

"If all had gone well?" Bridget looked at her, white-lipped.

"Sit down, *ma petite*. Now you will listen to me. A voice is a delicate thing. It needs to be pampered. Once in a lifetime you may find a Caruso who can abuse his voice without damaging it but," and she made an expressive gesture, "he was the exception. You have had a bronchial infection brought about by your own carelessness, and you got a rasping cough and talked when your throat was raw. I can understand that you lost your head when you found Liz Conway's body, but not even for a Liz Conway does a singer risk her voice. The voice must come first. So now you are not to sing for a month. Not a note. You are to rest and gain ten pounds and lie in the sun. Study your scores but silently. You can never understand a score too well. Now go away and come back to me in a month. Then—we shall see."

III

It was all very well to say, "You are to rest and gain ten pounds and lie in the sun." Bridget mentally reviewed her bank account. After sending a check to the hospital and paying the doctor she had exactly $864.42 on which to live, but she had no choice except to agree to Madame's terms. In time, of course, there would be the money Liz had bequeathed to her, but that might not be for months, depending on how long it took to settle the estate and to learn the truth about her murder.

Lie in the sun. Picking her way through icy slush at a curb, while a truck sprayed muddy water that drenched her stockings—her last pair, Bridget recalled —the idea seemed attractive, but winter vacations are for the rich.

Her legs were cold and wet from the muddy water

when she reached Fifth Avenue and went through revolving doors out of the bitter cold and into the perfumed warmth of a big department store. There was a mob at the stocking counter because of a sale, and she had to work her way through. She set her music scores with her handbag on the counter while she examined stockings.

She was in the street again, looking in the window at a wardrobe designed for a winter cruise to the Bahamas, when a hand touched her arm and a woman said, "Just a minute, miss." She was a square woman with a square face and a no-nonsense manner.

"What do you want?" Bridget asked in surprise.

"I think you know what I want." The woman showed a badge in the palm of her gloved hand.

"Police?" Bridget was bewildered.

"Store detective. Will you come with me, please?"

Bridget accompanied her helplessly and found herself facing a man who looked like what he was, a retired cop, but here apparently known as a security officer. The store detective took a pile of scores from under Bridget's unresisting arm and removed the three pairs of stockings that had been slipped between them.

"Have you a sales slip for these?"

"I didn't even know they were there. This is the pair I bought," and she took the package out of her handbag.

"Have you ever been convicted of shoplifting?"

"Of course not. And I didn't."

"Then how do you account for these stockings slipped in among the books?"

"Scores," Bridget corrected mechanically. "But I don't—" She pushed back the hood of her coat and thrust a hand through her hair. He wouldn't believe her, of course. People didn't. "Look here, I know how silly this sounds but I am being framed and I'm getting good and mad."

"Oh, come now, miss—"

"Evans. Bridget Evans. It's true. I can see it now. Last night someone doped me and planted a hypodermic in my room, and now this—and it's got to stop."

"Doped!" There was a queer tone in his voice. "And why do you think anyone would do that?"

"Because I saw a murderer and I can identify him. I should have realized that last night, but I've been ill and I was confused."

"Have you told the police about this murderer?"

"Of course. If you will get in touch with—his name is Carmichael and he's in the homicide division. I think he ought to know about this anyhow."

The security officer took a long look at her, startled out of his stolid calm. "Did you actually see her slip these stockings among her books?" he asked the store detective.

"No, I just saw them sticking out when she was walking down the aisle."

"Go ahead," Bridget urged him. "Please! Say it is Bridget Evans in the Conway case. He'll know."

He shrugged, made a call, talked in a low voice, looked again at Bridget, a different look, speculative, and hung up. "You're to stay here, right here, until he comes."

"Mr. Carmichael?"

"Mr.—oh, it seems he's a sergeant. No, it's a Lieutenant Baxter. He said not to take my eyes off you until he gets here."

"Good," Bridget said in relief. "At least nothing can happen to me while I am here."

IV

Lieutenant Baxter was taken aback. He had not expected anyone like Bridget Evans, and he hoped that Field's friend, Michael Graves, was not susceptible. Looked a bit dragged down by ill health but she was still something. Bad news for someone, Baxter thought cynically.

He had taken her over her story for the third time: the dope, the hypodermic, the shoplifting charge. Then he went back to the discovery of the body of Mrs. Elizabeth Conway.

"Are you still willing to identify the large young man, if we can find him?"

"I can hardly wait. I loved Liz Conway." Bridget, who had been sitting on the edge of her chair, sagged against it. "You don't believe me, do you?"

"I'm going to level with you, Miss Evans. Frankly, I don't know whether you are telling me the exact truth or lying your head off or a little of both. But at this point I can't take any chances on you. My department put you on the spot when that news story was released. If anything happens to you as a result of it the inspector will break a few of us. It's just that simple. You can't be any more concerned about your safety than I am."

Unexpectedly Bridget laughed and Baxter took a long breath. This girl was really something. "No hard feelings?" he asked.

"None at all, as long as you keep an eye on me."

"Meaning that I haven't done so well up to now, what with the doped drink and the shoplifting stunt?"

She nodded, her laughter fading. "I can't take much

more, Lieutenant. I can't take any more. I'm just plain
scared. And what baffles me is how these things are
done without my spotting the person who does them.
There's only one possible reason for this and that is to
discredit me if I'm ever called upon to make that identification. But the large young man is not around unless
he's invisible, and he was about the least invisible man
I ever encountered."

"Hasn't it ever occurred to you, Miss Evans, that
even killers have friends?"

She took a long breath. "Then it could be anyone."

"That's about the size of it. Unless, of course—" He
let the words drop into a pool of silence, watching the
ripple reach her.

"Unless I've lied all along and I'm doing this so you
will think I'm being framed. What it comes down to is
that the killer is either the large young man—or me.
That's what you mean, isn't it?"

Baxter relented. "It's not all that bad. There's an
obvious case against you—motive and opportunity. But
there are other possibilities. There's Conway's niece
who stands to inherit and hasn't put in an appearance,
in spite of the publicity we've given the Conway will.
She is assumed to have a real grudge against your
friend and a motive for wanting her dead. And at this
point," he knew he was a fool to tell her but something
about the girl made him want to reassure her, to take
that frightened look out of her eyes, "at this point the
case is wide open. Anyone could have got into the
building unnoticed Saturday afternoon. Anyone could
have been in the penthouse while you were there."

"Thank you for telling me, Lieutenant."

He got up. "I'll handle the shoplifting charge for
you. You can forget about that. And there's another
thing. An arrangement has been made to keep an eye

on you for your protection. So far I admit that it doesn't seem to have been very effective. But I can tell you frankly I wish to God that you were safely out of New York until we can settle this thing one way or another. It's a pity you can't go somewhere and lie in the sun."

And that was the second incident.

V

"If it wasn't for the hypodermic and that shoplifting deal, I wouldn't have let her go," the lieutenant told Mike over the telephone. "No, there were no prints on the hypodermic. By the way, that was a smart job for an amateur, getting her wine glass. We had the drugs analyzed, a barbiturate but not enough to kill. Of course, there's always the possibility she rigged both the hypodermic and the doped drink. People do queerer things every day."

"And the shoplifting?"

"I believe she was genuinely astonished about that, and it was so clumsy, the way they stuck out, unwrapped, between those books. Anyone trying to get away with them would have been more careful. And one thing I'm sure of: she wasn't lying about being frightened. Of course if she were the killer, she would have plenty to worry about."

Mike talked quickly, describing the result of his trip to New England and his call on Mrs. Briggs. "For my money, Miss Evans has been hounded all her life; I think that is what Mrs. Conway was trying to compensate for. She's honest, Lieutenant."

"She is also a damned attractive young woman, Graves. Smarter men than you have been misled by women with a lot less than her attractions."

"Well?"

"Well, watch your step. We're letting her go. Her doctor agrees that she should get away from New York. So be prepared to move. But remember this, she's not free, just on a nice long leash. I expect you to produce her when New York wants her back."

8

It seemed to Bridget that a lifetime had passed between her leaving Ma Baccante's house and her return to it. Perhaps the lingering weakness of her illness had distorted things, but when she remembered Madame Woolf's warning, the incredible shoplifting incident, and Lieutenant Baxter's advice and warning that she might be in danger, she felt that she had come to the end of her rope.

I suppose, she admitted to herself, I've always been a coward. There's nothing brave about me. *Killers have friends*. I'm afraid. I'm afraid.

When she opened the door of her room Mike Graves got up from the easy chair and put down the paperback edition of Edith Hamilton's *The Ever-Present Past*. Bridget realized that Peg had been right. Mike was an exceptionally attractive man.

"What do you think you are doing here?"

At her sharp tone, an eyebrow arched in surprise. "Waiting for you, of course, and incidentally improving my mind."

"After that business last night, all I need is to have someone find you lurking in my room."

"If you call that lurking, lady—"

"I'm serious, Mike. Just one more hint of scandal and I'll have to move. Ma won't put up with anything like that. And I simply can't afford to live anywhere else. This is really important to me."

He helped her with her coat, pushed her gently into the easy chair, and knelt to remove her boots. "Sit there and tell papa all about it. You've been getting yourself worked up, haven't you? Relax, lady."

"Oh, stop acting as though I were only ten years old."

He saw her expression and his tone changed. "What is it, youngster?"

"Mike, why did you take away that hypodermic last night?"

"Because I know a frame-up when I see one. I got the idea at dinner. You were doped and it must have been something in the Chianti, though I didn't spot it being put in your glass. So when I saw the evidence lying so carefully in plain sight on your dressing table, I thought the simplest thing would be to dispose of it. Someone is out to get you, lady. After this, keep your door locked to discourage prowlers."

"Like you?"

He grinned at her disarmingly. "You aren't very trusting, are you?"

"Up to now I haven't had much reason to be," she said in a tight little voice.

"I know that," he surprised her by saying. "Never mind, we'll work things out together."

"We will?"

"Of course. My dear old mother brought me up to look after damsels in distress. But we've got things to talk about while you are temporarily free of your two watchdogs."

"Have we?"

"You aren't very forthcoming, Bridget, considering that I've been urging you to confide in me and offered a shoulder for you to weep on. What brought you back here this afternoon, looking as though the hounds of hell were on your traces? I assumed Peg would be with you. She is certainly determined to keep the wolves at bay."

"You seem to forget that Peg has nursed me and looked after me. She has been incredibly kind."

"Incredibly. I distrust good samaritans on principle."

"It seems to be mutual. Peg distrusts you too."

"Well, well. I hope you aren't letting your natural good judgment be corrupted by a little prejudice." Before she could reply Mike dropped his bantering tone and touched her cold hand lightly. "What went wrong today?"

"Just about everything."

"That bad?"

She nodded.

"Tell me."

So she did, starting with Madame Woolf's decree that unless she went away for a month and lay in the sun she would not be able to continue singing lessons. Then came the preposterous shoplifting charge.

"Just what happened?" When Bridget had told him, he asked, "Didn't you see anyone near you at the stocking counter?"

"My dear man, there was a sale. People shoving, jammed together, and there was no attempt to hide the stockings. They were sticking out between the scores."

"Well, at least, we know it was a woman."

"How do we know that?"

"A stocking counter in a department store."

"There were quite a few men."

"Anyone you recognized?"

"No."

"And that's all?"

"All! Isn't that enough? Oh, the lieutenant who came to see me said that someone is supposed to be keeping an eye on me here. I don't know why and I don't know who."

"I hoped you wouldn't need to know."

Bridget stared at him. "You mean it is you?"

"Me. Or as my more grammatical friends would say, it was I."

"Are you police?"

He smiled then. "No."

"Then why?"

"Because my dear old mother asked me to. That was in the beginning. Of course, since then I've thought of another reason." When she made no comment his smile deepened. "What do you intend to do, Bridget?"

"I guess I'll go away somewhere but I don't know where, and I can't imagine how I can afford it. There will be the money from Liz Conway's estate some time —if I can convince the police I didn't murder her."

"Meantime you could borrow on your prospects."

"How?"

"From me."

"No! Don't ever suggest that again, Mike."

"Okay. Okay. Cool it, sister. No offense. But you know that Biblical phrase: 'Whither thou goest.' " He nodded at the question in her face. "Oh, yes, I'm going along."

"But you can't."

"Nothing can stop me." With a lazy finger he lifted her chin and made her meet his eyes. "I promise you that nothing will be done to embarrass you or damage your reputation, so you might as well get used to the idea. I intend to be where I can keep an eye on you, and I'll do a better job of it in the future than I've done in the past. That's another promise. But I'm going along.

It will be a lot easier and a lot pleasanter for us both if you'd accept the idea without fussing. You might even come to like it. We could get along awfully well, you know."

Bridget realized that it was true. Awfully well. "Why are you so insistent about coming along, Mike?"

"Because, whether I go or not, someone else is likely to. There's another saying: 'The bleating of the kid attracts the tiger.' At this point you are the kid."

"And who is the tiger?"

"I wish to God I knew. See you at dinner and remember to keep your door locked." He bent over and kissed her on the lips. It was quite a kiss. Then he went out and closed the door. "Lock it," he called.

She sat staring at the door, her lips parted. "Lock it," he called again impatiently, and she went across the room to turn the key in the lock. For some reason she no longer felt tired. Not tired at all.

II

When Bridget went down to the basement for dinner, locking her door, she heard Peg saying, "I can tell all of you right now that I believe in Bridget."

"There's no reason why you shouldn't," Mike replied.

There was an awkward silence as Bridget went to take her place at the table, the music students appearing to be intent on food, Mike and Peg watching each other like two strange and hostile dogs. Frank jumped to his feet when he caught sight of her, his face alight, and Bridget found herself smiling. His devotion was heartwarming but, as she could not feel anything more than gratitude for him, she wished he had picked someone else.

Ma brought her her salad and made no comment,

her eyes searching as she studied Bridget's face.

It was Peg who broke the silence. "How did the lesson go?"

"I didn't have one. Madame told me to go away and lie in the sun for a month and then come back. Meantime I'm not to sing a note or I'll risk ruining my voice altogether."

There was a different silence at the table. This was the kind of catastrophe they all understood.

"Where are you going?" Peg asked.

"I don't know. My reserve of money is just about exhausted. If I spend money for a trip, what will I live on when I come back?"

Ma was thoughtfully silent. She was proud of her students and fond of them, but it cost a lot to live these days and she couldn't afford to keep Bridget for nothing. No one would expect her to do so, though people were apt to be generous with other people's money.

After a moment's consideration Peg said, "It wouldn't take an awful lot. You're probably thinking in terms of one of those deluxe cruises they advertise, big plush hotels and people in evening clothes having caviar and champagne. Personally, the idea of lying in the sun in February makes my mouth water. If you'd be willing to travel cheaply, I'd be tempted to go with you. While my teacher is away I'm pretty much at a standstill."

Mike's knife halted and then he continued to cut his meat without looking up.

"Peg, do you mean it?"

"I'd go like a shot if you'd do it on the cheap—a bus instead of a plane and inexpensive lodgings. Come to my room after dinner and we'll talk it over."

"You're really going away?" Frank's face was blank with chagrin.

Bridget nodded. "I must. There's no choice."

"But I'd been counting on talking over my opera with you and consulting you about the soprano arias, all that. It's frightfully important to me."

"Lying in the sun is important to Bridget," Peg told him.

"Yes, I know, but—look here, can't I go along? It doesn't really matter where I work, and I wouldn't ask much, you know; just the odd hour when you had nothing to do. I wouldn't make a nuisance of myself." Aware of half a dozen pairs of amused eyes Frank blushed but he went on doggedly, "Do consider it. It's—well, when you read the score, you'll see that I've got something."

"Relevant," put in Heinrich, the erstwhile elevator operator, grinning.

As Bridget and Peg left the dining room together, Mike stood up and Bridget saw that he was not looking at her; he was watching Peg with narrowed eyes and a calculating expression she had not noticed before.

In her own room Peg gave Bridget the comfortable chair and sat on a straight one without touching the back, her hands relaxed on her lap. She looked down at her wool dress. "I get so tired of green. I wonder how many redheads have a yearning for pink or red, even when they know how grotesque they look." Without a change in tone she asked, "What's wrong, Bridget?"

Nothing but the fear of losing my voice, a shoplifting charge, a doping, a suspicion that I killed my best friend, and the warning that, if I am innocent of that, I am probably in danger from the killer—or his friends.

Aloud she said, "I was accused of shoplifting today."

"Bridget!"

When she had explained what had happened she said, "So I asked them to notify the homicide department, and they sent a man, a Lieutenant Baxter. And he said even killers have friends, and I'd be wise to go away for awhile. I'm just about scared out of my wits, Peg, and that's the shameful truth."

Peg leaned forward to touch Bridget's cheek lightly with a fingertip. "No fever. Well, let's plan. I've always thought the Valley of the Sun had an alluring sound."

"Where's that? It sounds like Egypt."

"Arizona."

"But that's twenty-five hundred miles away."

"We could take a bus. Suppose I look up schedules and we can get some travelers' checks and pack our bags and—remember to take summer clothing or light slacks and sweaters. We won't need much. Thank God for wash and wear. With luck we could be off tomorrow afternoon. We'll have to tell Ma, of course; maybe she could sublet our rooms for a month."

"What about Frank Saunders?"

Peg shrugged. "If he's so hell-bent on coming, actually it's not a bad idea. It's always handy to have a male escort, and I believe it's true that he wouldn't get underfoot. He's too obsessed by his opera to make a personal nuisance of himself. But let's not tell anyone else about our plans."

"Look, Peg, I'd better warn you; Mike Graves says he is going along, wherever I go."

Peg's lids shuttered her eyes. "I can't for the life of me see what he is up to. Not to denigrate your charms, honey, but you're not his type any more than I am. I'd expect him to fall for someone who is sleek and sophisticated. Does he claim that this is the grand passion?"

Bridget felt her face flaming and she was helpless to stop that betraying tide of color. "It isn't my charms that interest him."

Peg started to speak, hesitated. "We'll show Mr. Michael Graves—isn't his name familiar to you? I associate it with something but not music—a few tricks. In the morning we'll say that we'll be in for dinner as usual and then we'll get off in the afternoon very, very quietly. Okay?"

Bridget was silent.

"I'd better get busy," Peg said. "You run along and catch some sleep. But I wish—"

"Well?"

"I wish Mike hadn't taken that hypodermic. It's so —easy."

9

Bridget was the first in line behind the barrier, and, as soon as the door was open, she climbed on the big bus which stood panting in the long cold enclosure at the Port Authority Bus Terminal. Peg slid into the seat beside her, and Frank captured the aisle seat across from them. The bus filled quickly. And then, with a quiet, "Sorry," Mike Graves took the window seat beside Frank and sent a beaming smile at the two girls. "Dr. Livingstone, I believe."

The door closed and the bus was off. Around the curving ramp there was time for a breathtaking glimpse of the towers of midtown Manhattan, ablaze with light in the early winter dusk, and then the bus paused for a toll station and rocketed on, racing across icebound New Jersey, headed for Arizona and sunshine.

It was not until they stopped for dinner that there was any general conversation among the passengers. Up to that time each one remained within the solitude of his own mind. Bridget had tried to talk to Peg but the latter was unresponsive. She seemed withdrawn, her expression somber as though her thoughts were unpleasant. Bridget took a pocket score out of her handbag to read, shaping the notes in her mind, wondering in a kind of panic whether she would ever again be able to sing.

Dinner was at a hamburger stand, and for the first time the passengers took stock of each other, exchanged names and information as to where they came from and where they were going and the horrors of the worst winter on record.

A nervous woman passenger had been disturbing everyone because she was continually afraid that she had forgotten something and had to make a search of a carryall from which she refused to be parted. Now at the entrance to the hamburger stand, she dropped her handbag, and Mike stooped to gather up her scattered belongings. Before he could take the vacant stool next to Bridget, Frank appropriated it.

"I was stunned when Mike Graves showed up, cool as a cucumber, and pretending to be surprised. Is he following you, Bridget? Would you like me to have a word with him?"

In spite of herself Bridget was hard put not to laugh. The picture of Frank attempting to handle Mike boggled the imagination, but he was so deadly serious that she hastened to assure him that there was nothing to worry about.

"Well, just let me know if he is troublesome." There was something so cocksure about his youthful brashness that Bridget found him rather endearing.

"As long as you are around I won't be worried," she assured him.

Mike, standing behind her, touched Bridget's shoulder. "How's it going?"

"All right so far."

He waited as though expecting Frank to offer him his seat. Instead Frank gave the busy counterman his order and did not look up. Mike grinned. "Between Scylla and Charybdis," he murmured and found a place for himself farther down the counter but at a discreet distance from the troublesome woman passenger who had just dropped her menu in the soup.

Peg, still uncharacteristically somber, paid no attention to the lighthearted chatter between Bridget and Frank. When they piled into the bus again, there was a general shifting of position. People who had begun to talk in the hamburger stand were cultivating new acquaintances, finding new audiences for old stories and breaking through their isolation. Just how it was managed Bridget didn't know but Peg had the window seat beside Mike, who seemed determined to dispel her hostility and distrust, and Frank settled contentedly beside Bridget. Whether it was Mike or Frank who had maneuvered the change Bridget wasn't sure.

For an hour or so Frank sat beside her, talking of the opera on which he was working. It would be wonderful if Bridget could sing the leading role.

She laughed. "That would be like something in the movies. Young composers don't have their first opera put on at the Met, and young singers don't start out in leading roles. Anyhow I have a long way to go before I am ready for opera. It isn't just because of this setback, but I need much more training, more technique; I need to work harder on languages and, oh, so many things, besides learning the roles that suit my voice."

Now and then she looked curiously across the aisle. Mike was sitting turned away from her, engrossed in talk with Peg. Apparently he had succeeded in coaxing her out of her depression because Bridget could hear the other girl's spontaneous laughter.

There was nothing to see now but the lights of other vehicles—private cars and a number of transcontinental trucks rocketing across America on the great superhighway. After a while the ceiling lights were switched out, seats tilted back, and conversation dropped in a low-voiced trickle. Peg came back to resume her seat, and Frank left, saying, "See you in the morning."

"How did you get on with Mike?" Bridget asked curiously.

"Oh, fine. You can't pin him down to anything—slippery as an eel, but amusing. I have to give him that. Amusing and attractive—and does he know it!"

"What are you complaining about?"

"I'd like to know what that man is really up to."

The bus roared through the night at a steady seventy miles an hour. There was no sound but the throb of the motor, the swish of tires over wet asphalt, a deep rhythmic snoring from the fat man on the back seat, and the agitated twittering of the nervous woman who searched her handbag and her coat pockets for something. Bridget stared into the night and, beside her, unmoving, Peg was as wide awake as she was.

II

There is something about a transcontinental bus trip to break down the deepest reserve. People explained to each other why they took a bus instead of flying—"It's the only way to see the country, and you don't get hijacked to Cuba"—but no one suggested that it was also the cheapest way to travel. A third unattached male joined Mike and Frank in a friendly rivalry for Bridget's attention, and Peg watched them all, sometimes with amusement, sometimes with brooding intensity.

During the last day the scenery changed. There was no trace of snow. The ground was yellow and arid, the jagged hills were of reddish rock, unlike the gentler tree-covered slopes of the East, and, as they came closer to Phoenix, they began to see the giant cactus, the saguaro, standing forty-feet high, like headless men with arms uplifted to the dazzling blue of the sky.

As the bus slowed down, Peg said, "You won't need that heavy coat, the light one will be ample. It will be cool in the shade but the sun is blazing hot."

"I didn't know you'd ever been here before."

"I've read about it."

The bus came to a halt, and the driver shut off the motor. "Last stop, folks. Welcome to Phoenix in the Valley of the Sun."

He got out to distribute luggage, and the passengers drifted apart to go their separate ways after a chorus of good-byes and the exchange of addresses, which in a week would be lost or the identity of the owner forgotten. Finally there were only four people left: Bridget, Peg, Mike, and Frank.

"Well—" Mike began.

Peg interrupted. "Bridget, I've got the name of an inexpensive motel, only eight dollars a night, or ten dollars for two if we share a room."

"Fine," Bridget said.

"That suits my budget," Frank said.

"And mine." Mike grinned. "Just one big happy family." Blandly oblivious of the noticeable lack of enthusiasm in either Peg or Frank, he hailed a taxi and ushered them into it.

The motel was cheap, as Peg had claimed, but that was all that could be said for it. At least, Bridget thought, the sun was shining in Phoenix and, as Peg had prophesied, the sun was hot.

When they had paid for their rooms Mike suggested, "Why don't we have dinner together? Pick you up at six-thirty." He grinned mockingly at the hovering Frank. "Oh, come along if you like."

And Frank did like, though he was young enough to flush at Mike's grudging hospitality.

When the ill-assorted quartet was seated at Navarre's with cocktails in front of them, Mike raised his glass. "What shall we drink to?"

"Sunshine," Bridget said.

"The future," Peg said.

"Success," Frank said.

"Mission accomplished," Mike concluded. "And just why are you looking so pleased with yourself, Peg?"

"Just plain unbelieveable good luck!" she exclaimed. "Almost too good to be true." She pulled out of her handbag a piece of torn newsprint. "I picked up the local paper, looking for an inexpensive place for Bridget and me and—well, just listen to this:

> Live cheaply but high on the hog. Gourmet food. Charming rooms. Heated pool. Safe driver. Knowledgeable guide. Good company. Trips by hour, day or week on terms to be arranged. $75 a week. Call Latham.

"Too good to be true," Mike said, watching Peg.

Frank agreed. "There must be a catch in it somewhere."

"But we can't lose by asking," Bridget wailed. "Why even if it's only half as good as it sounds, I could afford to stay here for a month and still not run too dangerously short of cash when I get back to New York. I want to try."

"Then suppose I call them," Peg said.

"Why don't you let me case the joint first?" Mike

suggested. "You can't tell what a couple of girls might run into."

Bridget noticed that Frank was watching Mike with the same intentness with which Mike watched Peg. It only remained for Peg to start watching her for the wheel to come full circle.

"Why should you interfere?" Peg asked.

Mike's good nature seemed to be unruffled. "I can't believe in bargains, and I don't believe in buying a pig in a poke."

"This doesn't concern you, after all." For once the gloves were off.

"Oh, I'm in this, too," Mike said easily. "You might as well give up trying to lose me, Peg."

And then Frank intervened. "We're all in it together, aren't we, Bridget? It would be so much more fun doing things together."

After all, there was probably safety in numbers. "Why not?" Bridget said.

"Well?" Peg challenged Mike.

"Go ahead and make your call. But I can tell you how it sounds to me. There's a well-known invitation I've never cared for: 'Will you walk into my parlor, said the spider to the fly?' "

"All right, Mike, suppose you go ahead and make that call yourself if you're so suspicious. Go right ahead."

"I'll take you up on that." He reached for the ad.

III

Mike reported that Keith Latham was to pick them up at ten the next morning. He had to stop first to get someone from the Desert Hills Motel on Van Buren.

"You're sure you want to venture into this den of

thieves?" Peg asked mockingly.

"He sounded all right. Very Haavahd Yahd."

"I suppose you are Yale."

"Dartmouth. Come off it, Peg. After all, the first round goes to you."

"What did he mean by that?" Bridget asked Peg while they were preparing for bed.

"I don't know. Did you see his billfold when he was paying the dinner check? Those were hundreds, not tens or twenties. Anyone would think he had robbed a bank. Street artist?" Peg yawned. "What heaven to be able to sleep in a bed again." She switched off her light but now and then Bridget saw her hands move convulsively. She was still awake when Bridget fell asleep, and she was up and dressed by the time Bridget awakened in the morning.

"What kind of day is it?"

"The sun is shining, and the women are wearing cotton dresses with light coats."

"O frabjous day!"

When they had breakfasted at a drugstore counter, they returned to the dingy office of their motel to find Mike and Frank waiting for them, Mike reading a newspaper and Frank watching the door for Bridget.

A man in slacks and sport jacket, with a bronzed face under a shock of brown hair, a crooked nose, and a puckish mouth that turned up steeply at the corners, entered the lobby, looked around and came directly to them. "I am Keith Latham and, I devoutly hope, your future landlord, driver, guide, and what have you in your home away from home in Phoenix."

Mike performed the introductions.

"Have you checked out here? Then you had better take along your luggage. If you don't like our place, I'll bring it back for you."

When the bags had been stowed in the trunk of a big Cadillac, Keith said, "I have another prospect on the front seat. One of you can sit there with us and three in back. This is Oliver Putnam." There were more introductions.

Oliver was in his late twenties, strikingly good looking, with black hair and the pallor of a man who has had a long illness. He took one look at Bridget and moved over. "Plenty of room up here." When Bridget was settled beside him he declared, "This is my lucky day. What is your name? I didn't get it. . . . Oh, I think I've come across it before."

Bridget looked at him swiftly, looked away. Even in Phoenix there was no escape from the Conway case. Keith, she saw in relief, was a competent driver who did not fight for position on the road. He made no attempt to talk. Bridget was much too occupied in absorbing new impressions to make much response to Oliver's eager overtures. For the first time since Liz Conway's murder, her spirits were soaring. Phoenix was glittering modern buildings and wide avenues lined with palm trees; it was empty lots where the desert, yellow and bleak and tenacious, had reasserted its claim; it was people in bright dresses or slacks, in miniskirts or ruffled skirts that swept the ground. It was lean ranchers in wide hats and faded jeans; it was Mexicans and Indians in contemporary clothing and hippies in beaded jackets and headbands like the Indians of the past. It was space and dazzling blue sky and sunshine. It was summer in midwinter.

Keith turned into a carport big enough for three cars. The house, like the Cadillac, was unexpectedly luxurious, a long stucco building in the shape of an L that, with its grounds, took up most of a block. No attempt had been made to have a lawn. Instead, the spacious grounds acknowledged the supremacy of the desert. They were neatly graveled, with beds of cactus of a dozen varieties, a saguaro looming over the roof, a palo verde, orange trees, and squat palms like big pineapples.

The door was flung open by a tall girl wearing blue jeans and a red shirt, her blond hair tied back with a red ribbon. For a fleeting moment Bridget was aware of a sense of recognition and then decided that she must be wrong.

"This is Jean, my wife," Keith said. "These are—now let me see"—and he rattled off the names without a mistake.

Jean stood aside. "Come in." There was a long low living room with a baby grand piano, a record player, and bookshelves. There were couches and deep chairs. The draperies and carpeting were neutral, but the couches were upholstered in blue and the chairs in yellow, with one big leather reclining chair in crimson.

Mike looked around him with pleasure. "Now that's the way to fight back at the desert. Splash color all over the place."

"What a gay room!" Bridget exclaimed.

"That's what we were aiming at. Come see the rest. For those who like television there is this little soundproof room, then the powder room, the dining room, and the kitchen. The bedrooms are on the other side, air-conditioned, of course, though you won't need that for a while. There are five guest bedrooms but the problem is that there are only three bathrooms for the five. The pool is out here." Jean opened a door onto a big terrace gay with bright umbrellas and cushions, with plastic chairs and lounges, and a big pool that sparkled in the sun. "All the bedrooms open on the terrace so you can swim and go directly to your rooms to change."

Jean looked around. "I guess that is about all we have to sell except to say that Keith and the car would be at your disposal and that I'm a damned good cook. Oh, and we charge seventy-five dollars a week a person for room and board. The use of the car would be extra."

There was a moment's hesitation as though, Bridget thought, they were all waiting for something. "I'm going to stay," she declared, and there was a general chorus of assent.

"Oh, good! You choose your rooms and Keith will bring in the luggage. Anyone want a swim before lunch?"

Only Mike and Oliver Putnam did. Peg said, "I'd rather take a walk after so much sitting. What time is lunch?"

"One o'clock. Oh, there's another thing. If you want any drinks you'll have to provide them yourselves. They aren't included."

"I'll take care of that," Mike offered, and Peg gave him a long calculating look. "You name it and I'll get it."

"If you want a swim before lunch, I'll pick up the stuff," Keith suggested, and Mike made out a list at which Keith looked in surprise and gave him a hundred dollar bill.

Keith's brows shot up. "My God! If I start handing these out, people will think I'm the Phoenix Wizard."

"Who's that?"

"Remind me to tell you later."

When Bridget had unpacked her suitcase, she put on a scanty bathing suit and went out to lie on one of the lounges. Lie in the sun. That had been the prescription. The light was too bright to eyes accustomed to snow, the general grayness of winter, and the encroaching smog of great cities. She turned on her face, feeling the sun hot and healing on her back, compensating for the exhaustion that had followed pneumonia and the fatigue of the long bus trip. She stretched out and gave a little moan of pleasure. She was too content with sheer physical well-being to pay more than the most casual attention to the two men in the pool.

Mike was even bigger than she had supposed and a strong swimmer but without any particular style. He seemed as at home in the water as though it were his native element. Oliver Putnam was badly underweight and showed traces of illness. He floated on his back, eyes on the sky, his handsome face relaxed, at peace with his world.

Beyond the pool the fronds of a palm were motionless in the still air. An orange tree at the corner of the terrace displayed bright red fruit. Like a stage setting, Bridget thought. None of this is real; it's just a stage setting. I'll wake up and be in my room at Ma Baccante's with the sagging mattress on the bed or—but she shut out fiercely the memory of that other room, of the body of the woman with a noose around her neck. Violence had no place here.

Jean came out on the terrace and looked at the men in the pool. "Oliver," she called, for they had arrived at first-name terms immediately, "don't stay in the water too long. The sun is hotter than you realize and you can get a really painful burn before you know it is happening." She dropped into a chair beside Bridget. "Everything all right?"

Bridget, turning to face her, again had a fleeting impression of recognition. She also saw the expression on Jean Latham's face. Her hostess or landlady or whatever she was did not like her at all. It was an uncomfortable feeling.

"Everything is perfect. How can you bear to take strangers into this lovely place?"

"Well, we woke up one morning to discover that we had a big expensive car and a big expensive house and nothing to keep them up. We think that living should be fun; so we tried to figure out a way in which we could have fun and get someone else to pay for it, and I can cook and Keith can drive so—"

"But you charge so little. I shouldn't say that because I couldn't afford to stay here if it cost any more."

"This is our first experience at having paying guests, and we didn't want to scare anyone off. We can manage on this basis. If it works out we may raise our rates another year." Jean got up. "Well, have fun."

Frank came out of his room to take the chair Jean had vacated and to smile at Bridget in approval. "Maybe I'll be able to get you to myself now and then," he said, his eyes on the men in the pool.

"Aren't you going to swim?"

"I'd rather talk to you."

"But you can do that any time."

"Can I?" he said so somberly that she was disturbed. It would spoil things to have him genuinely in love with her. The wisest thing would be to ignore any emotional overtones. "Hey," she called to Oliver, "your face is turning a lovely pink. You'd better get out."

"Okay." He climbed regretfully out of the pool and went into his room.

Mike hauled himself up on the side of the pool nearest the lounge where Bridget was lying, his long legs dangling in the water, watching Frank in some amusement. "What price New York in February now?" Obviously he was not going to give Frank an opportunity to talk to her alone. He acted, Bridget thought, as though he was afraid to have her talk to anyone. "And what happened to your faithful watchdog?"

"Peg wanted to take a walk after riding so long."

"I'm surprised that she was willing to leave you alone, a poor helpless lamb among so many wolves."

"Stop riding Peg."

"I'll call a truce when she does."

Frank had fallen silent when Mike joined them, and now Oliver came out of his room in pale slacks and a gaudy shirt. He was, Bridget thought, quite the best-looking man she had ever seen. Actually they were all attractive in their different ways: Oliver with his dark coloring and finely chiseled features, Mike with his casual charm, Frank with his shy smile.

Oliver pulled up a chair to make a part of the group, while Frank glowered. "How wonderful! Think of being able to do that every day."

"Have you been ill?" Bridget asked.

"A long tiresome business but it's all over now. The only medication I need from here on out is sun and fresh air." He stretched his arms above his head and let them drop. "I seem to have come in late on this party. Are you four traveling together?"

Bridget explained that she and Peg were together and that Mike and Frank, learning of the inexpensive accommodations at the Latham house, had decided to join them in looking the place over.

"This is really something, isn't it?" Oliver said in a tone of satisfaction. "I couldn't believe my eyes when I saw that ad last night. I thought there was bound to be a catch in it. Then Keith showed up in a stunning Cadillac, you came out looking like a pint-size Venus, and now all this." He looked from Mike perched on the edge of the pool to Frank tenaciously near the lounge on which Bridget was lying. "Then you aren't married or anything," he said in a tone of satisfaction. "Now that's a perfect start for a vacation."

Mike came dripping out of the pool. "Don't you believe it. You're living in a fool's paradise."

"Competition?"

"And how!"

"I'm not the man to be conned out of the game that easily," Oliver declared laughing. "So far as I can see we are all on an equal footing, and the only old friend here is the red-headed gal."

"Oh, no," Peg said as she came out on the terrace. "Bridget and I met less than three weeks ago, but so many things have happened since then that we got to know each other in a hurry. So when Bridget had to leave New York, we joined forces."

"Had to leave?" Oliver asked in surprise.

"Oh, yes, didn't she tell you? Bridget stumbled into a murder and she's running away from the killer."

10

"Why did you do it?" Bridget asked. She had followed Peg into her room after lunch and watched while the latter brushed her red hair vigorously, making it crackle with electricity until it stood on end like threads of fire.

"To get a reaction. There's nothing like shock tactics. I wanted to catch Mike Graves off balance, just once, and see what he would do."

"What's behind this feud you're carrying on with Mike, Peg?"

"I don't know what he's told you, but he came out of nowhere to Ma Baccante's as soon as the news carried that story about your discovering Mrs. Conway's body. He was there when you got that dope in your Chianti, and he took away the hypodermic. He could just as well have put it there in the first place."

"Why?"

"Wanting someone to find it and believe you were an addict. And he could have staged the shoplifting deal. And he came on here to Arizona with us though we tried our best to give him the slip."

I didn't, Bridget thought, but she made no comment.

"Can't you see the thing looks wrong?"

"And yet, in a way, everything you've said about Mike applies to you too, Peg," Bridget said slowly.

"Heaven knows I'm not ungrateful for all you've done for me but you do see, don't you, that it could have been you?"

Peg met Bridget's eyes in the mirror. "Can you think of a single reason why I would do any of those things?"

"Well, if you should be a friend of the killer, you might have intended to discredit me so no one would believe my identification of him."

"And why do you think I came out here with you?"

"I don't know. Mike thinks—"

"And of course you believe anything Mike says."

"I don't know what to believe. But I must say, Peg, I think the strangest thing of all is that there was so little reaction to that comment about my running away from a killer."

She remembered that Keith had come out on the terrace with his arms filled with bottles. Jean had followed him, bringing a tray with glasses, a bowl of ice, a mixing pitcher, and a shaker. When Peg had made her dramatic announcement, there was a moment when they had all been frozen in position like figures in a wax museum.

"We'll set up this table as a sort of permanent bar," Jean told her husband. "You put the bottles here and Mike can be bartender. Okay?"

"Okay," Mike said. He put coasters on the table near them. As Oliver came to sit beside Bridget as a kind of tacit indication that he was on her side, Mike dropped a plastic coaster.

Oliver bent over to pick it up and put it down for Bridget. "There you are, lady," he said, smiling at her.

"Martinis for everyone?" Mike asked.

"Not for me, thanks," Jean told him. "The cook shouldn't drink."

"Of course she should." He pressed a frosty glass into

her hand. "How about you, Frank?"

"Fine." He took the glass and looked from Bridget to Oliver and went to sit sulkily beside Peg.

The first reference to Peg's startling statement was made by Keith Latham and then almost as an afterthought. "Running away from a killer. Personally I'm delighted to have a little excitement in our lives; Jean and I have got in a rut."

"It's not as funny as you seem to think," Bridget told him.

"At least no one can hurt you here," Frank said in a belligerent tone.

"So you are that Bridget Evans," Oliver said. "I heard the story on the radio. It's a hell of a thing to happen, but I'm glad it brought you here, right into my orbit."

"Well," Jean said, "you can be sure no large young man is going to hurt you in this house." Again Bridget was aware that the other girl disliked her. "This is a law-abiding community."

"Not all the time," her husband said. "We've had our moments. Let's drink to the Phoenix Wizard, the man who made crime pay."

"Who is this Phoenix Wizard?" Mike asked.

Keith laughed. "That's quite a saga. A Chicago guy came out here, one of those slick con men, lured by the story of the annual search that goes on in the desert for a famous lost gold mine. Like everyone else he failed to find it."

"This is new to me," Mike said.

"Years ago a guy died after discovering a fabulous gold mine and once a year a search is made on the desert for the lost mine. People hunt in groups, because if you get lost on the desert, you are apt to die of dehydration if nothing worse. But he did manage to get his filthy paws on some land that had been left unoccupied to provide the town with plenty of breathing space instead of living elbow to elbow. Our bright guy found a loophole in the zoning law and he turned the property into a sort of miniature Disneyland—spoiled the whole section so that property values went down and people sold out at a loss, and who got their property dirt cheap? He did.

"He was easily the most hated man in Phoenix. Public Enemy Number One. Everyone was praying for the time when he would slip up and, of course, he did; some crooked real estate deal. He was tried and sent up for five years to the cheers of the public, but it took a while for us to savor the full beauty of the situation. He had to have a public defender because he was broke."

Keith laughed and nodded when Mike held out the pitcher. Peg covered her glass quickly. "You wouldn't be trying to get us tight, would you?"

"Go on with this fascinating tale," Mike said.

"Well," and Keith laughed again, "it turned out that this comedian used another guy to collect money for him to keep himself in the clear. Just before the balloon went up, the other fellow disappeared, and the money went with him in hundred-dollar bills. Some reporter referred to him as the Phoenix Wizard and the name stuck. He was picked up later on some charge and got a year's sentence but there was no money on him. So the story got around that it is cached somewhere near Phoenix. Anyhow, there isn't a week when parties don't go on a treasure hunt for the guy's hoard."

"That's quite a tale," Mike said. "How much of it do you believe?"

Keith shrugged. "I don't know. There may be something in it. I like the idea that the bastard who put up that poor man's Disneyland and destroyed property values should fall for another con man who raked in all the money."

"There's a kind of justice in it," Oliver admitted.

"You seem to feel," Frank said, "that crime should go unpunished."

"I didn't say that." Oliver was not perturbed by Frank's disapproval. "Let's say I take a relaxed view of it, unless it is violent. I dislike violence. Which brings us back to Bridget's murder. Why do you think your friend was killed, sweetie? Hate, gain, revenge?"

"That's the only possibility I can see, but it would have to be the work of a disordered mind, where Liz was concerned. Everyone—"

"I know," Peg interrupted. "Everyone loved Liz. Except the one who hated her. Let's face it, someone wanted her dead. Someone tightened the noose around her neck—"

"Don't!"

Keith set down his glass and got to his feet, standing with his hands at his sides like a butler. "Luncheon is served," he announced gravely.

II

In the drugstore telephone booth Mike called Lieutenant Baxter. "I don't like the feel of this thing. Can you check on these people for me? I sent you fingerprints of the whole lot by airmail this afternoon on some plastic coasters. They are labeled."

"You've got the wind up. Why?"

"I have a hunch we've been led into a sweet little trap, though it's a mink-lined trap, if that's any comfort. Here are the names. Ready?"

"Go ahead. What do you want?"

"Background. Financial standing. Previous records—. if any." Before he rang off Mike asked, "Any word yet on Snodgrass or the missing niece?"

"Nothing yet."

"Queer about the girl, isn't it? Are you sure there isn't a letter from her in Mrs. Conway's files?"

"Mrs. Conway didn't keep personal letters."

"Oh, hell! By the way, you might get a lead to Snodgrass by checking on shoe-repair places. That's the only way he has of earning a living."

"Will do. You're worried about the situation, aren't you? Keep an eye on the girl."

"I'll do my best."

"It had better be good. You are responsible for her to the department."

III

Next morning the whole party strolled through the Botanical Gardens.

"I don't like the feel of this thing," Frank said.

After some preliminary skirmishing with Oliver and Mike, he had attached himself firmly to Bridget, and they walked side by side along a narrow path that could not accommodate a third person; no one in his right mind disobeys the frequent signs warning: KEEP ON THE PATH. Among the less desirable denizens of Arizona are poisonous snakes, lizards, and spiders such as tarantulas, and scorpions. It's nice to be able to see what is coming. The varieties of cactus in Arizona are highly improbable, and the party moved at a leisurely pace, identifying such odd things as the upside down tree.

"Why," Frank asked, his voice cautiously low, "did Peg bring out that story of your flight from a murderer in such a melodramatic way?"

"She said she wanted to get a reaction."

Behind them Oliver walked with Peg, while Mike followed with Keith. Once Bridget heard Mike ask some idle question about Harvard and knew that he still distrusted the whole Latham deal as he had done from the time Peg had discovered the ad. Will you walk into my parlor, he had said. But unless this was Bluebeard's chamber, what on earth was there to be afraid of in this charming house with its charming hosts?

Frank took her arm in a proprietary way. "I'm going to have my work cut out," he grumbled, "the way Mike and Oliver keep trying to get you. I can't always hold them off."

He was proved right about that when Oliver took advantage of a general pause to read a sign. He took Bridget's arm and steered her away. "You're so hedged in," he complained, "that I can't seem to get near you, and I want to put in some sound work at developing a beautiful relationship. How about doing something wild, a riotous debauch like going to the movies with me?"

"Well—"

Seeing her hesitation Oliver smiled. "Nothing up my sleeve. You'll be safe with me. After all, what could happen to you at the movies?"

Mike had come up so quietly that neither of them had noticed him. "Now that is definitely an idea. Let's all go to the movies."

And that is how it was done. While the Lathams cleared away the dinner dishes, Mike called a cab and the five paying guests were off to the movies.

"For sheer effrontery," Oliver commented to Bridget, "Mike takes the prize," but he seemed to be more amused than annoyed. "He's definitely a guy to be reckoned with, but I know a trick that's worth two of that."

As the usher led them to their seats, he put his hand on Bridget's arm, restraining her. Then, when Peg was seated between Mike and Frank, Oliver put Bridget in the seat next to the aisle in the row behind. As both Mike and Frank craned in the darkness to find them, he grinned.

"Okay," he whispered when the movie was well under way, "here we go. Careful now. No disturbance."

They slipped out without notice.

"Am I being kidnapped?" Bridget asked.

"You are. I found a good place to dance."

"But there are no cruising taxis around here."

"You underestimate me, sweetie." Oliver pointed proudly to the taxi waiting at the door. "I had a word with him before we came into the theater." He looked so triumphant that Bridget laughed.

The orchestra was good and so were the drinks. Oliver proved himself to be a superb dancer.

"I don't dance well," Bridget warned him. "I've had so little opportunity."

His eyes warmed as he looked at her. "That's all over now; you'll dance well with me." Whether or not it was his skillful lead, she did dance well. Oliver was a gay companion and she felt more lighthearted than she had in weeks. They talked and laughed and danced and laughed and sipped their drinks and laughed. Once while they were dancing, Bridget looked up to see Oliver smiling down at her.

"You look like a happy man," she said impulsively.

"At this moment I am. It can be a good life, sweetie. You know you ought to be full of laughter, but you wear a 'keep off' sign like that cactus we saw today with the deadly spines. Someone must have hurt you very much."

His manner was unexpectedly gentle.

It was only when she yawned that Oliver laughed and called for his check. "Time you were getting to bed, sweetie."

The taxi left them at the Latham house. An outside lamp was burning and the porch light was on. The rest of the house was dark.

"How do we get in?" Bridget whispered. "I don't want to awaken the whole house."

"I asked Keith for a key."

"You think of everything, don't you?"

"Not always. But where you are concerned, I believe I could learn to." He bent over and kissed her lightly. "Good night, sweetie."

"Good night, Oliver. Thank you for a lovely evening. Bridget closed her bedroom door and groped for the light switch, and out of the darkness a man lunged for her, caught her in his arms so tightly that her face was smothered against his chest and she could make no sound.

"Where the hell have you been?" Mike muttered. "What happened to you?"

She pushed him away with all her strength, her heart thudding from the fright he had given her. "What are you doing here?" Her voice was low. On one side was Peg's bedroom with Frank's on the other. Her French window opened on the terrace.

"What did Oliver want?"

"He wanted to take me dancing and he did and I had the happiest evening I can remember until you spoiled it. Now get out!"

"You damned little fool! You don't know this guy; you don't know anything about him. And even after the police warned you that you were in danger, you went off with him. Anything could have happened."

"Well, nothing did, except that I had a good time with an attractive man with nice manners and gentle ways. And anyhow he's the only one here who couldn't be a danger to me, when you come right down to it. It was only accidentally we met him, and he had nothing to do with Liz Conway."

"You don't know that. You don't know where he came from."

"That applies to you too, doesn't it, Mike?"

"Don't be an idiot. The way you sneaked out——"

"It was the only way we could get rid of you," Bridget said sweetly.

"Oh!" For once Mike was at a loss. Then his anger returned. "Okay. So he's a good-looking guy with nice manners. And what else do you know about him? If you can't see he's as phony as a three-dollar bill there's something wrong with your head."

"I know as much about him as I do about you, and I like him a whole lot better."

"You are making that fairly obvious. I wish to God we hadn't come to this place. It's like walking into a trap. I don't like it, with every room opening on the terrace. Tomorrow I'll get you a bolt for your window. Anyone can get in from the terrace. That's the way I came tonight."

"But I can't take liberties with the Latham house."

"You'll do as I tell you!"

"You——" The rest of the sentence was smothered by Mike's mouth on hers. Then he said, oddly breathless, "Lock your door," and he was gone.

11

The temperature dropped in the night from the seventy-five of the evening before to forty, and it was still chilly enough in the morning so that the paying guests dug into their wardrobes for sweaters.

"Who," Keith inquired idly at the breakfast table, "is the hardy stargazer who spent the night on the terrace?"

Frank looked up alertly.

"Sorry if I messed things up," Mike said. "I find it is the best way to lick insomnia."

Oliver looked from Mike to Bridget, a smile deepening at the corners of his mouth.

"That was a nice trick you and Oliver played on us last night," Peg said. "When the lights went up I had all I could do to keep my two escorts from starting a search party. A thing like that undermines a girl's self-confidence."

"When I take my girl out," Oliver said, "I don't believe in making it a community affair."

"Your girl?" There was an edge on Frank's voice.

Aware of the impending storm, Oliver switched the subject adroitly. "Look here, time is a-waning and there are lots of things I want to see out here. I'm the world's most tireless sight-seer. How about Wickenburg, that typical old western mining town, according to the information I picked up in my motel? Can we get there from here?"

Something changed in Keith's face. Though what was wrong with Oliver's suggestion Bridget didn't know. Frank too was aware of Keith's hesitation and looked at him quickly.

"Why, yes, of course," Keith said after a pause. "Only thing is that there's really nothing much to see, even of the famous dude ranches scattered all around the place. It isn't like Old Tucson where daily entertainment, including scattered gun shots, is set up for tourists."

"I read something about Gold Rush Days," Oliver persisted. "When's that?"

Keith's reluctance was evident to everyone now. "Oh, yes, there's a carnival and parade and rodeo and the public is allowed to pan gold the way they did in the old days. That's rather fun."

"Real gold?" Oliver asked, and Keith laughed.

"Oh, they just salt the dirt for fun. You get a few flakes the size of a pinhead, and there are always a couple of the old miners around for local color."

"When is this going to be?"

"This weekend." Again Keith's reluctance was noticeable.

Oliver looked around him. "How about it?"

"Oh, why not?" Keith capitulated. "I'll drive you. If we leave early, we can be in time for the parade, have lunch at the Gold Nugget, do some gold panning, and get home in time for a dip before dinner."

Bridget, looking at the puckish face that had been made for smiling and that was not smiling now, thought: he'll drive us because he wants to make sure where we go and what we see.

"And there is Oak Creek Canyon," said the tireless

sight-seer. "I understand that is one of the great beauty spots."

"It is. We'll certainly put that on the agenda." Keith was more enthusiastic. "Any more ideas?"

"Am I the only one with suggestions?" Oliver asked. "Are there any of the old Indian cliff dwellings around here or are they all in New Mexico?"

"Sure, we have one of the best of the lot, Montezuma's Castle. It isn't a castle and Montezuma never heard of it, but it is an authentic old cliff dwelling that gives a fairly clear idea of how people actually lived in it. We can take that in on our way back from Oak Creek Canyon."

"Any errands?" Keith asked. "I'm off to do the family shopping."

"You could give me a lift, if you will," Mike said. "Main post office."

"If the house is being cleared, I am going to practice," and Peg went into the living room.

"I've been neglecting my work," Frank said and went to his own room.

Oliver lingered for a moment with Bridget, but Jean was putting soiled dishes on a trolley in a leisurely way, and he drifted off to change for the pool.

Then Jean turned to Bridget. "You have every man in the place eating out of your hand. Mike and Frank are ready to tear Oliver apart because he slipped off with you last night."

"But they have no right to object to what I do."

Jean gave her a long look, and again Bridget had a curious sense of recognition. "I have just one thing to say: Keith is mine. Hands off."

Bridget was torn between indignation and an impulse to break into exasperated laughter. "I don't take what isn't mine."

"Don't you?"

The color rose in a slow tide over Bridget's face and then she turned on her heel and went storming into the living room where Peg sat at the piano, her voice rising and falling in scales. She broke off abruptly when she saw Bridget's expression.

"What's wrong?"

"I'm not staying here one more day."

"Why?"

"Jean practically accused me of making passes at Keith and she warned me off. Mike made a scene last night, because Oliver took me dancing, and I'll bet Frank is waiting on the terrace right now to do the same thing. What's wrong with everyone? I'm going to take the first bus for New York."

"You," Peg said calmly, "are going to sit down and listen to a few well-chosen words of common sense. In the first place, your teacher wanted you to come here to save your voice. In the second place, the police wanted you to come here to save yourself. In the third place, you have already paid a month's room and board in advance and you can't find any place as cheap as this and you certainly can't afford the risk of going home in the cold weather. In the fourth place, you seem to be a potential bombshell where men are concerned and the sooner you learn to cope with that fact, the better. Just the same, you were a fool to slip off with Oliver last night."

"What's supposed to be wrong with Oliver, anyhow?"

"I don't know." As Bridget was about to explode, Peg said, "Quiet down, honey. Mike and Frank were all set to go off like a high explosive last night when you disappeared with Oliver; I know you say they have no rights in the matter. Okay. But you are in a nasty spot, and you don't know a thing about this Oliver Putnam. Oh, he's good looking and gay and he has obviously fallen for you in a big way, but still—"

"I know he can smile and smile and be a villain, only I don't believe it. And all this fuss is ridiculous."

"What was the deal about Mike sleeping on the terrace last night? Is he protecting your virtue or threatening it?"

"God knows. It probably had nothing to do with me; all I know is that he doesn't like this setup."

"What setup?"

"The Lathams, the Cadillac, the house. The Lathams need paying guests the way they need a second head."

"People can be over-extended and need ready cash."

"Mike thinks the whole thing is a trap we've walked into."

"Nuts. But I would give a lot to guess what Mike really thinks. And just give me one cogent reason why the Lathams would take in five people to feed and house if they didn't need to. Don't be a little donkey, Bridget. Obey orders and go out and lie in the sun and try to keep your young men under better control." Peg patted Bridget's cheek and then gave her a little push toward the door. Even before Bridget had closed it behind her, she heard Peg's warm contralto at work on scales.

II

As she had expected, Frank was waiting for her on the terrace. "Why on earth did you do it, Bridget? Go off with Oliver last night?"

"Oh, what difference does it make?"

"I'm so worried about you I can't concentrate on my own work. My mind is just a blank when I try to compose."

"I'm sorry."

"And it makes a big difference to me, not just for the sake of my opera." Frank's face was flushed and his manner solemn. "When Oliver called you his girl, I was pretty sick."

"I'm not anyone's girl. Let's get that clear, Frank. And Oliver was just needling you and Mike. Let's not talk about it any longer."

Oliver came out on the terrace, wearing red trunks, and sat down on the edge of the pool to apply suntan lotion with a lavish hand. Then with an amused look at Frank, grimly seated beside Bridget, he slipped over the side of the pool, relaxing from the chill in the air by the warmth of the heated water and then floating on his back, eyes closed. Once again Bridget thought of him as a happy man. Of all the people in the Latham house, he was the one wholly content with his lot, the only one without a trace of wariness or hostility or suspicion.

Now Peg had abandoned scales and she began to sing Delilah's *"Mon coeur s'ouvre à ta voix"* in a rich, warm contralto.

"That should be your song," Oliver said.

"But I'm a soprano."

He smiled. "That's not what I meant," and the smile deepened when she did not ask him to amplify.

"In a few weeks I'll be able to practice again. I can hardly wait."

"Does it matter so much?" Frank asked.

"It matters terribly. More than anything in the world. I think I'd do anything to be able to sing, to sing really well, I mean."

Oliver scrambled out of the pool and stood shivering in the cool air. "What's happened to that much-publicized Arizona sunshine?"

"After all," Jean said defensively, as she came out on the terrace, "it's only February. We're probably in for a few chilly days and then it will be warm again. You're getting a chill, Oliver, and you're much too thin to withstand cold. Go in and take a hot shower and give yourself a good rubdown."

"Right you are, but when I've gained fifteen pounds on your cooking, which I fully expect to do, I'll be able to chop the ice before I dive in." He ran into his room and in a few minutes they heard the shower running.

The temperature was still low by evening, and Keith got a chemical log for the fireplace in the living room where they had all gathered. Mike and Frank were playing gin rummy, and Keith asked Peg to select a record. When it proved to be Vivaldi, Oliver stretched out his hand to Bridget.

"This," he said, "is where we lowbrows retire to sink our minds in some television." In the small soundproof room, he collapsed in laughter on the couch. "Their faces!" he gasped. "Oh, lord, it was funny. Now I suppose they think I am seducing you."

"More likely that I am seducing you," Bridget retorted. "Believe it or not, Jean Latham thinks I'm a femme fatale."

"So does anyone in his right mind. The only surprise is that you haven't discovered that for yourself, unless you've been living in a convent."

"I might as well have been."

"But that," and again Oliver smiled at her, "is all over now. From here on out things are going to be different for you. Ever had your fortune told?" He took her hand and scrutinized it carefully. "I see a big change coming in your life. I see fame and fortune and travel with a dark-haired man and sunshine and a good life and a lot of laughter and—I'm in love with you, Bridget." The laughter still lurked but he was serious.

"Please, Oliver!"

He looked at her, a wry smile tugging at his lips, and then he bent to kiss the palm of her hand before he released it. "I can wait. I'm very patient, sweetie, and I've learned how to wait for what I want. And anyhow I don't want a reluctant or an uncertain bride. I want you to come a-running."

"Why you—" she exclaimed indignantly, and then they were both laughing.

That was when Keith opened the door. If he noticed that the television set had not been turned on, he made no comment. "Jean's had one of her better ideas. Hot spiced rum punch. We can't have it often because it requires a cool evening; in fact, the colder the better. Come along and join us."

Jean waved cheerfully from the table where she was stirring the contents of a large steaming punch bowl from which an aromatic odor of rum and lemon and cinnamon sticks and other spices arose. She filled a punch cup and turned the handle toward Bridget. "Careful. It's scalding hot."

Bridget cautiously lifted it to her lips and burned her mouth with the hot liquid. She set her cup on a table. "I'll have to let it cool a bit."

Whether it was the invigorating effect of the hot rum punch or not Keith said, "Get some wraps and we can dance on the terrace. The floor is waxed and there is a full moon."

Bridget and the other girls provided themselves with sweaters while Keith stacked dance records on the player and did not turn on the terrace lights. Bridget found herself dancing with Oliver and then with Mike who wasn't so good and then with Frank who wasn't good at all and was embarrassed about it and then with Keith who was very good. But she didn't worry about Jean's jealousy. She didn't worry about anything. She was young and happy and dancing in the moonlight, and between dances there were sips of the rum punch that was never allowed to cool completely before Jean refilled her cup.

12

The boy sat at the wheel of the low sports car, one hand on the wheel, an arm around the girl who was wedged as close to him as she could get, her head on his shoulder, a marijuana cigarette in her hand. Alternately she lifted it to her lips and to his.

"This is living it up," he said.

"Where did you get the car, Harold?"

He laughed. "Believe it or not, this jerk left it parked outside a night spot with the key in it. And a full tank."

She took a final puff of the cigarette and freed herself from his hold to press it out in the ashtray. "He'll report it to the police," she said uneasily. "And you don't want to get picked up again."

"We got lots of time. He was just going in when I spotted it. Coupla hours yet, at least. It's some baby, isn't it? I betcha it could do a hundred miles an hour easy." He put his foot down on the gas and the car shot forward as though it had been fired out of a gun. The boy wasn't prepared for the power or the speed and for a moment he was startled. Then as it occurred to him that the power was his, he felt exultant and pressed his foot to the floor. The needle went up from seventy to eighty to ninety.

Beside him the girl laughed and snuggled against him again. His arm went around her. They were winged.

The world was theirs. Ahead there were flashing lights and the boy eyed them, puzzled. His long hair blew in his face and for a moment shut off his vision.

There was a scream of tires, a crash of metal, a flash of brilliant light, and the boy and girl were inextricably merged with the tangled metal and consumed by a leaping flame.

The truck driver shut off his motor and ran back sobbing, "Oh, God! Oh, God" while he tried futilely to approach the blazing sports car.

It would have to be a dark street where he couldn't get help before his own gas tank went up. But unexpectedly there were lights and running feet.

"Stand back!" Someone caught the truck driver's arm. "Get the hell away from here. You can't help. The whole thing is going up. Jean, call the fire department and an ambulance. Mike, you'll find a fire extinguisher on the wall of the terrace. Okay, fella, come along with me. You're in shock and you don't know it. Give me a hand with him, Oliver."

"Can I help? My name is Roon. Dr. Roon. I've got an emergency case across the street, but I can leave him for a while. Yes, get that truck driver into the house. And no alcohol. Keep him warm if you can. We can't help those poor devils now, even if they are still alive. Oh, quick work!" There was the beep-beep of a fire engine coming around the corner, followed by an ambulance and a police car. The street, which five minutes earlier had been dark and deserted except for a speeding sports car holding two hopped-up youngsters getting a thrill and living it up, seemed to be filled with people in every possible state of dress and undress, some of them with flashlights, all of them, except for the professionals, getting in the way of the men who were trying to do the work.

"Leave it to us," one of the firemen implored Mike, who was wielding the fire extinguisher he had brought from the terrace.

"Stand back," a policeman said. "Why don't all you people go home to bed?"

But no right-thinking person can go home to bed while a fire blazes. Even the crumpled frame of the sports car, which had smashed its way into the side of the truck, had its morbid fascination.

"Where's the truck driver?" the policeman demanded.

"In the big house," Mike told him. "The name is Latham. There was a doctor who had an emergency call across the street, and he's taking a look at him."

"Hurt? There's an ambulance here."

"I don't think so. Just shock. Come on in and talk to him."

In the Latham living room, the whole party had gathered. The doctor looked over the dazed truck driver who kept shaking his head and muttering, "Jeez! I couldn't help it. I was halfway across the street, see, and this car came right at the side of the truck. Must have been doing a hundred miles an hour. I couldn't move fast enough to clear it. He hit the side of the truck. Jeez! Those poor guys inside. Those poor guys. I couldn't help it." And in a moment he began all over again.

As there were more beep-beeps, they crowded to the windows and saw another fire engine slowing at the wreck.

"Nothing you can do," the doctor said in a comfortingly reassuring voice. He looked around. "Can anyone take this man home?" As the truck driver protested, he said, "It will require a wrecker to get the truck free, and, anyhow, you shouldn't drive tonight. You're in shock."

The policeman got his name and address. "All right for me to go?" the driver asked.

"Sure. We can get your story in detail tomorrow. I don't see how anyone can blame you."

"You don't know my boss. Once you get the insurance boys asking questions, he turns the air blue."

"You're in the clear on this," the policeman told him.

"I'll drive him home," Keith offered. "No trouble at all."

The two men went out, following the policeman and the doctor who, yawning widely, said he must return to his patient.

And then at last the fire was out and a wrecker arrived to haul away what was left of the sports car and to remove what remained of a young couple. This was not a pleasant or a very complete and tidy job. Identification was impossible. It was even difficult to determine the sex of the victims.

And at length the fire engines left, with a muted beep-beep because there was no further need for haste, and the police car pursued its way with a wary eye for people loitering and an ear tuned to the radio with its constant reports of man-made disaster and disturbances, and an ambulance bore away mangled flesh that had lived up a lifetime in one flaming moment, and the street was silent again as though the crash had never happened.

II

That was when Mike looked around the living room: Jean, in a thin robe over a short nightgown, her fair hair tied back with a red ribbon, her nose shiny and looking too big for her face; Peg trim and collected in a tightly belted green flannel robe; Oliver with trousers and sweater pulled over his pajamas; Frank who had dressed hastily and untidily.

"Where is Bridget?" As they stared at Mike he explained, "No one could have slept through that uproar. What's happened to her?"

"What could happen to her?" Jean asked rather tartly, but Mike was running down the hall, knocking on Bridget's door, calling her, then banging. He raced through his own room and out onto the terrace and at length they heard him unlock her door.

They were all crowding in the hallway now. "What's wrong?"

Without a reply Mike jerked Bridget brutally out of bed, shook her, and slapped her face, shouting furiously at her.

She tried to pull away, to shake him off. "Lemme lone," she muttered.

"Bridget!" He slapped her again so hard that Peg winced in sympathy.

"What's wrong with her?" Jean asked, looking from Mike to the girl in the transparent nightgown, whose head lolled forward.

Mike shook her. "The kid has been drugged. If that doctor hasn't gone, get him over here and make some coffee. Strong and black. No, you don't," he exclaimed as Bridget sagged in his arms. "Walk!" He put his arm around her waist and dragged her across the bedroom, stumbling, kicking a chair out of the way.

"Frank," Jean said, "you're the only one who is dressed. Run across the street and try to get that doctor. Otherwise we'll take her to a hospital. I don't want anything happening to her here."

"But it's all right if it happens somewhere else," Mike said, his expression ugly.

"You look after Bridget." Frank went outside and they could hear him running.

"People will think that this is bedlam," Jean said as she went out to the kitchen to make coffee.

Peg came to take Bridget's arm and keep her walking. "What is it?" The freckles stood out on her face but her manner was as calm as always.

"Some barbiturate, at a guess; probably in that rum punch. It was so highly flavored anything like that would be completely disguised."

"Or she might have taken it herself," Peg said. "After all, we did find that hypodermic in her room at Ma Baccante's."

"So we did," he said pleasantly.

"But you took it away."

"For the record I did not dope Bridget either at Ma Baccante's or here tonight."

"Then who did?" As Bridget swayed against her, Peg nearly lost her balance.

"Bridget!" Mike shouted in her ear. He shook her until her head bobbed up and down helplessly, and she opened her eyes to protest, "Lemme lone."

"Keep awake!"

"Then who did?" Peg repeated as they resumed their staggering walk, dragging the unconscious girl along.

"Anyone. She left her punch cup on the table while she was dancing, as we all did."

"Someone here then?"

"I would assume that was obvious to the meanest intelligence, which yours is not. It narrows the field, doesn't it?"

"Here, let me help." Oliver came to take Peg's place and the latter dropped down on the side of the bed. "Thank God, it occurred to you to check on her."

"No one could possibly have slept through that uproar, the crash and the fire engines and the police and all the commotion. So she had to be missing or dead or drugged." As Bridget's head sagged and her eyes closed, Mike slapped her cheek so hard she whimpered.

"You're a cold-blooded devil," Oliver said.

"Not as cold-blooded as the person who did this to Bridget. Any barbiturate in quantity combined with alcohol—my God! She was never intended to wake up. Get that into your head, man. Someone around here is playing for keeps."

"Or," Oliver said quietly, "someone thought it a clever ploy to wake her up in the nick of time, make a good impression, and get rid of the competition. It would be a nice gambit." His hand tightened on Bridget's arm. "Keep walking, sweetie. You're going to be as right as rain."

Jean came in with a pot of coffee and a cup. She looked from the girl in the transparent gown to the men on either side of her, her lips tightening. Then she looked at Peg who seemed to be almost as stunned as the doped girl, like someone who has miscalculated badly.

"How is she doing?"

The front door opened and Keith came in, saw the girl staggering between the two men, saw his wife pouring a cup of coffee. "What in God's name has happened now?"

"Explanations later." Mike was curt. "Let's have a cup of that coffee."

Frank flung open the door. "I brought the doctor. How is she?"

The doctor looked around the room and went to raise Bridget's eyelids and take her pulse. He waved away the coffee. "We won't want that." He handed Frank his car keys. "It's the blue Plymouth in the driveway across the street. In the trunk you'll find a stomach pump. Needed it this afternoon for another would-be suicide. Sometimes I wonder why we bother to save them."

"This isn't attempted suicide," Mike told him; "this is attempted murder."

The doctor gave him a startled look. "Clear the room. I need someone to help me. No, none of you," as Keith, Mike and Oliver volunteered.

"I'll help," Peg said, and, when Frank came in with the stomach pump, she pushed them all out of the room and closed the door.

For the next half hour, the Lathams and three of their paying guests sat in the living room drinking the coffee Jean had prepared for Bridget, wondering how she had got the dope but no longer denying, as they had been inclined to do at first, the possibility that murder had been intended.

"The stuff was in the punch," Mike said. "It had to be."

"But how would anyone be sure which was her cup? Perhaps the whole thing was a ghastly accident," Keith said.

"Of course, it would be easy enough to watch where she put it," Frank said thoughtfully, "but where—" He got up, wandered around the room and out on the terrace. "Where's the light switch out here?" he called and Keith turned on the terrace lights.

"What are you looking for?"

"The punch cups. That's funny. The punch bowl is still on the table but where are the cups?"

The veins in Keith's face stood out. "Just what are you implying?"

"What Mike told the doctor—attempted murder by drugs of some sort in the punch. Where are the cups?"

As Keith lunged for Frank, Oliver pulled him back. "For God's sake, let's have no more melodrama to-night." His face was white and drawn.

"Oliver is right," Mike said, "but so is Frank. Where are the punch cups? The doctor will want to know. So will the police."

"The police!" Keith exclaimed.

"If Bridget wants them. She's the one who has a right to call the tune. After all, she's the one who is fighting for her life at this very minute."

"All right, let's find the damned cups," Keith agreed.

There was no problem. The punch cups, washed and polished, were lined up neatly on the drainboard in the kitchen. And, unexpectedly and shockingly, Jean began to scream. Keith reached her first and shook her hard. "Snap out of it or I'll pitch a glass of water at you."

She caught her breath, held it, got herself under control, and then began to cry soundlessly, the tears streaming down her face, which looked distorted and ugly. Keith sat beside her on the couch, his arm around her, repeating over and over meaninglessly, "Okay, darling; okay, darling."

And at length she lay quietly against him. "I never had hysterics before," she said in a surprised tone.

"It's a wonder to me," Oliver said, "that we aren't all in hysterics after a night like this. I could do with a good cry myself." He won a tremulous smile from Jean. Then the smile faded. She got up, shaking off her husband's arm. "But I didn't do it," she said fiercely. "I didn't dope Bridget's punch cup. I didn't wash the cups. I didn't! I went straight to bed when the rest of you did. Didn't I, Keith? And I fell asleep at once. And when the crash woke me up, I went to the window and saw the flames and ran out. Keith got there first and we were together until we were told to get out of the way and we came back here to the house, bringing that poor distraught truck driver."

"The point is," Frank said, "that in all the confusion anyone could have gathered up the cups without being noticed and washed them to do away with any evidence. How many of you know where anyone was during those ten minutes?"

Keith thought about it. "Well, I saw Jean, of course, and Mike came out and then went back to get the fire extinguisher from the terrace. I don't remember about anyone else except the doctor."

"I saw Mike running with the extinguisher," Jean said. "But I didn't notice him again. Peg was in the living room when we came back, and Oliver was outside and came back for his sweater. Peg didn't go out, because she figured we'd just be in the way. She was watching from a window."

"What it boils down to," Mike said bluntly, "is that not one of us has an alibi that is worth a damn."

"I suppose that is important," Oliver said, "but right now all that matters is how Bridget is making out."

"There's nothing you can do, Oliver," Jean told him. "You look half-dead yourself. Better go to bed."

"I want to be sure that she is all right. She's my girl."

"Peg will look after Bridget."

"Will she?" Frank asked suddenly. Like the others

he was bleached with strain and shock and fatigue. "What do we know about Peg, after all, except that she never willingly lets Bridget out of her sight, and she steered her out here like a homing pigeon where this could happen?"

"Damn it," Keith exploded, "do you think Jean and I—"

"Cool it." Mike turned as the doctor came into the room. "Is she—?"

"The patient will be all right. Cleaned her out. She's exhausted and she will need to rest. Let her. I can guarantee there's no dope in her now. But I've taken some samples." His expression was grim as he probed face after face. "Miss Reston has been a tower of strength, and she has promised to spend the rest of the night—it's four o'clock now—in her room."

"No!" Mike and Oliver and Frank all spoke at the same time.

"Unless Miss Reston is mentally unstable, she won't take a chance on injuring my patient tonight, even if she was responsible for what happened to her." Dr. Roon stretched wearily. "Quite an active neighborhood you live in."

Mike picked up the doctor's bag and the stomach pump. "I'll take these for you. How about the crash victims?"

"Good God! There wasn't enough left that was recognizable to make a post mortem possible. I've seen bad things but that is one of the worst. Good night. I'll be across the street with my patient, but I hope to God you won't need me again. Even doctors like to sleep when they get the chance."

"Well," Keith said, "off to bed with you, Jean darling."

"I ought to speak to Peg, to see whether there is anything I can do."

"She'll tell you if she needs anything, and you can take over for her tomorrow while she catches up on sleep."

Oliver said a weary, "Good night," and went into his room.

Frank went to his room, took a blanket and pillow from his bed and went out on the terrace. He pulled a lounge close to Bridget's window and lay down, wrapped in his blanket.

A few minutes later Mike came out, also equipped with blanket and pillow.

"I'm on guard," Frank said.

Mike grinned, his face drawn with fatigue. "We'll make it a community project." He pulled up another lounge.

13

It was noon when Bridget raised heavy eyelids. She had never felt as tired as this in her life, even after a serious illness. There was a vague impression that she had had a horrible nightmare. She remembered farther back. She had been dancing with Oliver who said that he loved her and that he would wait until she came a-running. She found herself smiling. There was something irresistible about Oliver, good looking and gay and a wonderful dancer and both gentle and understanding in his attitude toward her. It would be easy to become very fond of Oliver.

Memory stopped there. She could not remember how the evening had ended, could not remember going to bed.

As she shifted her position, she was aware of sore abdominal muscles. There began to stir a vague impression of being forced to walk up and down, of Mike shaking her and slapping her, of having unpleasant things done to her helpless body, and of being agonizingly sick.

She tried to read her watch face and decided that she could not focus on anything smaller than Big Ben. What on earth was wrong with her?

She sat up, astonished to realize how weak she was, and saw Peg asleep in the easy chair with her knees over the arm. It took a long time to puzzle out this phenomenon. Then Bridget caught sight of Jean outside the French window, trying to peer in. While Bridget stared at her, frowning in bewilderment at this extraordinary behavior, Jean slipped into the room, glanced at the sleeping Peg, and put her finger to her lips.

"You all right?" Her lips shaped the words.

Bridget nodded.

As though aware of her presence, Peg opened her eyes and sat up. She seemed to come fully awake without any time for adjustment. She looked at Bridget. "How do you feel?"

"Like hell warmed over," Bridget said frankly. "Did you spend the night here?"

"What was left of it."

"I'll bring Bridget a tray," Jean said, "and you go to bed, Peg. I'll take over."

"Not until I've had something to eat. What time—oh, lord, it's high noon."

"I'll bring you both trays," Jean said. "Before I went to bed last night I made a fresh pot of coffee and put out some doughnuts and anyone who wanted some this morning could help himself. About eleven, when I finally managed to crawl out of bed, I served a kind of brunch." She chuckled. "You ought to have been the best-guarded girl in Arizona last night, Bridget. Peg was in your room, and both Frank and Mike were staked out on the terrace outside your window. Keith found them there this morning when he went out to take a dip in the pool and help wake himself up."

"What's this all about?" Bridget demanded, pulling herself up on her pillows.

"Last night there was a terrible automobile crash down the street. One car burned up. We had two fire engines and an ambulance and a police car. It was pretty dreadful. Two people were killed."

"How horrible!"

"They saved your life," Peg told her somberly. "When it was all over, Mike got upset because you hadn't put in an appearance. He said no one could sleep through that, so he broke into your room from the terrace and found you unconscious. According to a doctor, who had been on an emergency call across the street, you had a massive dose of some barbiturate dissolved in your rum punch."

Bridget lay back on her pillow, wordless.

"Well, Mike and Oliver and I walked you and kept you awake until Frank brought the doctor who pumped you out. If you hadn't been found when you were, you would have been dead by now."

"That's the second time," Bridget said. "The second time." She tossed back the sheet.

"You stay where you are. Doctor's orders. Bed today, and we won't talk any more until you've been fortified by having something to eat. Then I'll go to bed and catch up on sleep. Will you be all right while I take a shower?"

Bridget nodded without speaking and stared at the ceiling while Peg went to shower and came back, looking composed but with the freckles prominent on her colorless face and her green eyes somber. It wasn't until Peg brought her a damp washcloth, a hairbrush, and a mirror that Bridget saw her own shadowed and sunken eyes looking huge in her white face.

Jean looked haggard too, Bridget thought, when she came in, pushing a trolley that held breakfast trays, a coffee pot, and an extra cup for herself. When she had adjusted Bridget's tray, Jean filled her coffee cup. Bridget lifted it slowly, set it back in its saucer, and met

Jean's eyes. The latter's face flamed with color.

"All right," she said abruptly. "I suppose Peg has told you. You got sleeping pills dissolved in your punch cup. It's the only way the thing could have happened, and I made the punch and Frank found the cups all washed and polished in the kitchen and no one could remember where anyone else was during all the excitement, except that Keith and I were together, and I don't expect you to believe that, and I did warn you away from Keith and—well, there it is."

There was a moment of strained silence and then Bridget raised her cup.

After Jean's outburst no one spoke until Peg and Bridget had finished eating. Then Jean collected the trays, looking down at Bridget who looked back at her. She had not realized before how tall Jean was, what a challenging manner she had.

When she saw that Bridget was not going to speak, Jean went out of the room.

II

The other time, Bridget thought, I was doped to discredit me. It wasn't meant to be murder. This was. This is what Lieutenant Baxter was afraid of. And there is only one possible reason: I can identify the man who killed Liz Conway and killers have friends. A friend here in this house. Which of them tried to silence me permanently: Mike, Peg, Frank, Oliver, or the Lathams —individually or together?

But Mike had kept her awake until the doctor came, and Peg had helped the doctor take care of her. No matter how she looked at it, the thing did not make sense. Granted that either Peg or Mike was working for the killer why would they then save her life? But it couldn't be Mike. He had come here to look after her, with the knowledge of the police, and he had been genuinely terrified for her when she had slipped off to go dancing with Oliver. That was why he had been so angry.

The Lathams? Jean was jealous of her. Jean had made the punch and kept Bridget's cup filled, and she had disliked her from the beginning. If only, Bridget thought, she could remember where she had seen Jean before. And Keith had suggested dancing on the terrace and her cup was left lying around. Mike had believed from the beginning that Peg had steered Bridget to Phoenix and straight to the Latham house. *Will you walk into my parlor?*

As soon as she had regained enough strength to get around, she would return to New York, and this time she would go alone. But flight, she realized, was no guarantee of safety. She would be in danger in New York too.

I don't know what to do, Bridget admitted. I don't know what to do. Somehow I don't want to run away. If I do that, I'll always be afraid. I'd rather stay and face whatever comes, and I'll be careful not to drink anything other people don't drink.

After a while she fell into an uneasy doze. And Jean pulled a chair up to the table near her window on the terrace and began to shell peas for dinner, waving away the anxious whispered queries of Frank and Oliver and Mike.

III

Keith came out on the terrace, making a great creaking noise by trying to walk on tiptoe, and sat on the floor beside his wife, his hands clasped around his knees, his head resting against her thigh. "How is Bridget?"

"Exhausted, of course, but she'll make it all right."

"She had better," he said grimly.

"What do you mean by that?"

"You know what I mean. The situation has changed, hasn't it? The whole picture has changed. It's the hell of a mess now, and it needs a whole new script."

"You think we made a mistake, Keith?"

"Someone did, and now, frankly, I don't know what to do."

IV

Peg, in spite of bone-breaking fatigue, lay sleepless in her darkened room. She had closed the French windows and pulled the draperies across, but still the brilliant sunlight came through and the shadow of a palm tree was black against the light drapery. Even through the closed window the sound of a mockingbird running through its repertory was clear and sweet.

Everything had gone wrong, she thought. How could it have happened when she had planned so carefully? Everything had gone wrong. She had blundered. If it had not been for the car crash, Bridget would be dead now. Who could have foreseen that? She shivered.

Out on the terrace Jean and Keith were whispering. They were frightened too, as badly shaken as she was, and she had made a mistake. Perhaps a fatal mistake.

I don't know what to do, Peg thought.

V

Mike dug into his pocket for more coins and let them rattle into the pay phone. While he waited, he kept an eye out for customers in the drugstore, though none of them seemed to be interested in him. When his call came he talked fast.

"Last night someone attempted to murder Bridget Evans by an overdose of some barbiturate. . . . Of course it was intentional." He described the discovery of her drugged condition. "Oh, I explained the whole setup to the doctor and he is sending his report on to you and samples for your own laboratory to test. . . . Anything new on Snodgrass?"

"A lead. We're following up today."

"How about Mrs. Conway's niece with her grudges?"

"No luck so far. Look here, Graves, if you can't guarantee that girl's safety, we'll have her brought back here in protective custody. Have you any plans?"

"I don't know what to do," Mike admitted.

VI

Frank watched Mike as he opened the door of the telephone booth and moved behind a revolving stand of paperback books. Mike, for once, was shaken out of his usual casual and relaxed manner. He looked profoundly worried.

Frank waited until Mike had left the drugstore and then he sauntered after him, a boyish figure who might have been any carefree winter tourist, except for the eyes that never left their quarry.

I don't know what to do, Frank thought.

VII

When Jean refused to let him speak to Bridget, who was resting, Oliver shrugged and went out for an aimless walk. That had been a close call last night, a terrifyingly close call.

In periods of enforced inaction, Oliver had learned to discipline his thoughts. As he strolled along the street he deliberately tried to put Bridget out of his mind and to concentrate on the scenery around him: Camelback mountain crouching redly in the sunlight, the mass of Squaw Peak, the elaborate houses of Paradise Valley perched like mountain goats on narrow ledges, looking out over the encroaching smog that was coming even to the desert; a modern house followed by a corral of horses—Phoenix was the only city he knew where horseback riders were a commonplace; a lawn kept green by underground irrigation followed by a wide patch of empty desert or an orange grove. Phoenix was not crowded; it was a city of space.

Perhaps, after all, it would be a pleasant idea to settle in Phoenix or on a nearby ranch. That would be a good life. Plenty of action out-of-doors. Would Bridget like such a life? No, the idea was to forget about Bridget. He was not a marrying man and Bridget— it would be fatal. Bridget was a jinx. He wasn't superstitious but he was not going to be jinxed. Not he. Why in hell had he fallen for her of all people? But the damnable thing, he admitted, was that he had fallen for her, hook, line, and sinker. And it was going to change everything.

If it hadn't been for the horrible death of two young people and Mike's alertness, Bridget would be dead. Dead and gone. It was only when he had taken Peg's place to help walk Bridget that he had known that he could not let her die. Jinx or whatever, he wanted her.

It's always the unexpected that upsets the apple cart. Back to the drawing board, Putnam. Only I don't know what to do.

14

Lieutenant Baxter looked up as Carmichael came into the small cubbyhole that passed for an office and shook snow off his overcoat before he hung it up.

"I'm going to get some of those fleece-lined woolen gloves," the sergeant said as he blew on his hands. "No warmth in this other stuff."

"Take your time," Baxter said. "At your convenience you might report on where you've been."

Carmichael was aggrieved. "I'll write it up in a few minutes, as soon as my hands are warm. I left a note for you."

"Anything on the Snodgrass man?"

"I've been checking on shoe-repair shops. I must have interviewed fifty of them in the last two days, but I ran him down this morning. Little place only a few blocks from where he used to live, on the edge of the Village."

"Did he explain why he ran away?"

"He didn't run away. This son of his stole the money he had put aside for expenses, and he had to give up his own business. He's working for another guy now, and has a room over the shop."

"Well?"

"Well, he doesn't know where his son is and he's mighty anxious."

"Afraid he's out robbing someone else?"

"Afraid of what he might do. Apparently he took with him those sleeping pills his sister had been collecting."

"Good God! There was an attempt to kill Bridget Evans last night with sleeping pills. I've just been talking with Graves."

"So you think Snodgrass is out there." Carmichael sneezed.

"I can't see two people trying to kill that girl. I'll wire Graves to get her back here on the next flight."

"Did you see that report from the Phoenix police?"

"What report?"

"The one I gave—oh, I hadn't finished typing it. I had to go out to get a flu shot. It's here somewhere." Carmichael pawed over papers.

"Give me the gist of it." Baxter controlled his rising temper with an effort. "You can type it up later."

"That check you wanted made on the people in Phoenix. The cop I talked to said Keith Latham needed paying guests the way he needs a case of shingles. Well-to-do guy from the East, got a bullet in a lung in Vietnam and has to live in a warm, dry climate. Owns a big house, has a sound bank account, a considerable amount in investments, according to his broker, and a big ranch near Wickenburg. Nothing against him. He and his wife are a popular young couple, married two years ago. Before her marriage she was Jean Barbara Reston."

"Reston? Reston! That's the name of the girl who, Graves believes, steered Bridget Evans out to Phoenix."

"Reston isn't a common name. I wonder—sisters, perhaps? But that doesn't explain anything, does it?"

"It just raises more questions. If Peg Reston is related in some way to Mrs. Latham why didn't she say so?

Why this paying-guest setup? Get me Graves in Phoenix, Carmichael."

"You know, Lieutenant, I can't buy the idea that the Reston girl is guilty. I'm damned if I can. And you notice there's no large young man in this outfit and that's what you'd expect Bridget Evans to be afraid of, if she told the truth."

"If I were Bridget Evans, I'd be afraid of my own shadow," Baxter admitted, "the way things are."

"If she's innocent."

"If, of course, she is innocent. Any report yet on that stuff Graves sent airmail with fingerprints of the whole party?"

"Not yet. I sent it down to be processed." Carmichael sneezed. "I shouldn't have waited so long for that flu shot." Seeing Baxter's exasperation he added hastily, "Someone killed Mrs. Conway. That's one fact no one can deny. Up to now we don't seem to have a case against anyone."

"We've got some queer specimens to account for. One is this Peg Reston who appeared at Mrs. Baccante's boarding house right after the story—your story—about Miss Evans was released. She keeps an eye on Miss Evans, steers her like a homing pigeon to the Lathams' house in Phoenix and never lets out a peep about the fact that Mrs. Latham may be related to her. And Graves discovered the Latham ad for paying guests appeared only the one time, so it looks like a trap set up to catch the Evans girl. What are they up to, Carmichael? I wish we had a trained man there instead of Graves. He's obviously so besotted by the girl that he can't be objective. That comes through in everything he says. Get me the Phoenix police. Then find out what's been done to trace that niece, though I can't for the life of me see how she could get involved with the Phoenix setup. Unless something breaks at once I'm going to have Miss Evans brought back to New York where we can keep her safe."

Carmichael sneezed.

II

"So what are you going to do?" Mike asked.

"I don't know," Bridget admitted.

So far, it seemed to her, the prescription had failed badly. She was on the terrace again, lying in the sun with two people there. Whose arrangement it was she did not know but whenever she left her room there were always two people with her. At the moment Peg was lying on the other lounge, eyes closed. She might be asleep; she might be listening to that low-voiced conversation. None of it seemed to matter.

"I've talked to Lieutenant Baxter of the New York police," Mike said, his voice pitched to reach only her ears. "He doesn't think much of the way I've been protecting you. He says he wants me to bring you back to New York or he'll have someone else do it, to make sure you're safe."

"I wasn't safe there either, was I?" Bridget said dully. "Sooner or later he'll get me, either by himself or through one of his friends."

"You're talking about the large young man?"

"Yes, and don't laugh at me, please."

"I'm not laughing. You're in a panic, aren't you?" His hand closed over hers, held it tightly.

"Sometimes I can't help feeling that I am getting what I deserved. The punishment fits the crime, you know."

"I don't know, and what nonsense is this?" Mike's voice was louder than it had been. Peg's eyelids flickered though she did not raise them.

"I never told you about the girl who came to see Liz Conway. Her name was Louisa Snodgrass. She was a pretty kid, about my age or maybe a little older and—eager. Like a little child outside a toyshop window on Christmas Eve. Everything was wonderful and it was all going to happen to her. I'd been spending the afternoon with Liz, singing some Mozart, while she explained the role and made it come alive for me. We'd been working together for some time before Isabella came in to say that this Miss Snodgrass had been waiting quite a while—so she had overheard how kind Liz was to me.

"Well, she asked Liz to hear her sing, almost begged her. And Liz was always patient, though she was annoyed at this girl for having got past Isabella, because she never wanted to see strangers except by appointment. You can understand that. People who force their way in always want something and they are hard to get rid of.

"Anyhow, the girl sang, of all things, the "Bell Song" from *Lakmé,* and it was—oh, dear, it was ghastly. She didn't know how to breathe; she had no technique; her range wasn't equal to it. If it hadn't been so sad, it would have been comic. But it mattered terribly to her and when she finished you could almost see that she was waiting for waves of applause from the Met audience and someone in the balcony shouting 'Bravo!' and there was just silence, and then Liz tried to let her down—oh, gently. But the girl couldn't believe she wasn't great. She wouldn't believe it. She said it was unfair. She said I was taking what belonged to her.

"Well, she went away at last, crying and carrying on, and the next day she killed herself and left a note—"

"I know about the note. She blamed Mrs. Conway."

"And me."

"Well?" Mike's grip on her hand tightened. With his other hand he tipped back her head. "Well, Bridget? Mrs. Conway was too honest to feel guilty, wasn't she? Wasn't she?" he repeated. "And yet you blame yourself. Why?"

"Because—"

He looked at the apparently sleeping Peg and bent over, brushing Bridget's cheek with his lips. "Because you've always been blamed when things went wrong. You're in the clear on this, and Mrs. Conway would be the first to tell you so. You've got to be proud of yourself, as proud as I am of you. Whatever happened to the Snodgrass girl had nothing to do with you."

"But there is still the large, young man. I feel sure he is the Snodgrass girl's brother. No one else could conceivably want Liz to die. And if he killed Liz, he'll want to kill me too."

"What are you going to do?"

"I'm scared, Mike; I'm scared to death. But running away is no good. I've tried that before. What you run from always runs after. I'd rather stay here and face it."

"That's my girl." Forgetful of Peg's presence—awake or asleep—Mike bent over and kissed Bridget on the mouth. "We'll fight it out on this line if it takes all winter."

15

It was Oliver who once more brought up the matter of the sightseeing excursion to Wickenburg where Gold Rush Days would be celebrated with a parade, rodeo, gold panning, and assorted amusements.

"Well," Keith began with notable reluctance.

"Let's take a vote on it," Oliver insisted.

"Aye," Frank said promptly.

"Oh, let's do something," Bridget exclaimed.

"All right with me," Mike agreed.

"If all the rest of you are going, I'll go too," Peg said.

"I'll stay home and arrange something especially nice for dinner when you get back," Jean told them.

When Bridget came out of her room, wearing a rust-colored slack suit, she saw Jean and Keith talking quietly on the terrace. When they saw her they almost sprang apart.

"I like gals who are prompt," Keith said, smiling in approval. "You're looking like yourself now, Bridget. And turning a nice golden brown. Very becoming. A few more days of Arizona sunshine and you'll be a new woman."

"That would be all to the good. I am sick and tired of the old one."

"I can name a couple of guys—three guys—who

seem to approve of the original model," Keith told her. "In fact, if the truth must be told, four guys."

Bridget looked hastily at Jean, but the latter returned the look, smiling.

For the first time since their arrival everyone seemed to be in a holiday mood, and the talk was easy and relaxed and gay on the trip to Wickenburg, which lived up to expectations. "But I didn't know," Bridget exclaimed in delight, "that places like this were real. I thought they were just settings for western movies."

Frank drew her carefully out of the street as the parade came in sight—floats with pretty girls, Indians in full regalia careening along, cowboys, dudes from the ranches, their tailoring impeccable, their boots polished, their habits perfectly fitted, a sprinkling of old miners, survivals of the gold rush days in Wickenburg, bearded and looking, Bridget said, as though they too had stepped out of the movies.

"And those rugged-looking cowboys. But no wonder with the hard lives they have."

"We aren't living in 1880," Keith told her. "When you see those guys risking their lives in the rodeo, it is rarely because of the prize money. It will be for the hell of it. Most of them are college graduates. Some of them own their own string of horses and their own ranches. A few of them travel to rodeos in their own planes. Not at all like the movies."

It was all colorful and good fun. As the crowd grew thicker and pressed to the edge of the sidewalk for a view of the parade, the party was forced to separate. Only Frank and Oliver kept close to Bridget, shielding her from the crowd, watchful of anyone who came too close. She felt lighthearted and carefree. The sun was so hot on her back that she took off her light jacket with a sense of liberation. "The first spring day without a coat is the nicest in the whole year. And think of having it come in February."

"You're lovely when you are happy," Oliver told her. "I wish I could make you so all the time."

She smiled at him, grateful for his admiration, accepting it as one more element in a sunlit warm day, and he was aware that that was all the meaning it had for her.

A fierce-looking Indian, his face painted, feathers in his hair, a bow slung over his bare back and a bunch of arrows thrust into his belt, was pretending to career into the crowd, uttering a savage howl, proudly holding before him in the saddle a papoose with coal-black eyes who thought he was in control of the big horse.

When the last of the parade had gone by, the people on horseback exchanging greetings with the watchers on the sidewalk, Oliver said, "Now how about some gold panning?"

"I'd rather walk around the town," Bridget said. "I've never seen a truly western small town before. Where are the others?"

"That's what I was wondering," Frank said. "I saw Mike a while ago, standing back against a building. He's tall enough to see over most of the crowd. Oh, there's Keith."

Keith waved as he caught sight of them. "How'd you like it? Let's go do some gold panning. It's great fun."

When Bridget saw the long tables and the intent people shaking their pans, dipping water into them, shaking again, she balked. "No. Not in that heat. I'm going back to the western museum where it is dim and cool and sit down. You can pick me up there when you are ready."

"Let's all go to the museum?"

"I wish you wouldn't. I want you to do what you would have done if I hadn't come." Bridget was so firm that the men turned away, though she was aware that Keith was not pleased.

The museum enchanted her but it was a small place and she had soon exhausted its possibilities. She wandered up the stairs and out onto the street, wishing she had worn a hat. The sun was relentless at high noon and she was aware that her head had begun to ache.

She wandered down a side street where she found a patch of shade with a bench. She sat, half-asleep, idle thoughts drifting through her mind. It was some time before she became aware of the voices. At first they were indistinguishable murmurs and she paid little attention until she saw the black shadows on the ground and she was aware of the man and woman locked in each other's arms. Embarrassed, she was on the point of coughing to announce her presence, when she heard the woman saying, "Darling, darling, darling," and it was Peg's voice.

Bridget stirred and turned her head cautiously. The man and woman were behind the thick trunk of a giant oak tree.

"I can't stand this any longer, sweetheart," the man said. "Just talking to you on the telephone, hiding on Keith's ranch. The hell with it. I'm coming out."

"You can't, dear. You can't. You mustn't. You'll ruin everything."

"Everything is shot to hell anyhow, it seems to me," the man said somberly. Bridget, shrinking back as deep into the shadow as she could get, saw the couple break apart, saw the man straighten, saw the great height and bulk, saw the jutting nose. And screamed.

Mike was beside her. It did not occur to her to wonder where he had come from. It seemed inevitable that

179

he should be where she needed him when she needed him. That had been implicit between them for a long time.

"Bridget, what happened to you?"

She pointed to the couple who stood as though frozen. "The large young man."

Peg was chalk white, the freckles standing out on her face, but she raised her head proudly, slipped her hand through the arm of her companion. "This is my husband."

His hand closed over hers, holding it firmly. "My name is John Reston. It's about time I came out of hiding. I've been letting my wife hold the bag long enough." He looked from Mike to Bridget and his brows shot up. "I've seen you before."

"Outside Liz Conway's apartment."

"So that's it. You are Bridget Evans who made a present of me to the police. And you?"

"Michael Graves."

"What part are you playing in this charade?"

"That question is for you to answer, isn't it." Mike looked at Bridget. "Are you sure?"

She had clutched at his arm but her voice was level. "I'm sure. This is the man I saw when Liz was murdered."

"All right," Reston said, "that's true enough, but I didn't kill her. In fact, I never saw her. I have never seen her in my life."

"But that's impossible," Bridget said.

"I told you," Peg wailed. "I warned you, Jack. There's no way you can convince her."

"Is that why," and Bridget's eyes were wide and startled, "is that why you tried to kill me, Peg?"

"Hold it!" Mike said. "Let's sit down here in the shade and have a talk. But all the truth this time, Peg.

Up to now you've been lying your head off, haven't you?"

She took a long breath and expelled it with a small despairing gesture. "It's just—you won't believe us. I know you won't believe us."

"Try and see," Mike suggested.

"Bridget is so sure she can't be mistaken."

"Bridget," Mike pointed out, "has been in the hell of a spot. She has been doped and has had fake evidence planted in her room and had a charge of shoplifting laid against her and been nearly killed with sleeping pills—so nearly killed that—"

"I didn't do that!" Peg said.

"But you did put dope in the Chianti; you did plant that hypodermic in her room; you did put those stockings in between the scores so the store detective could hardly help seeing them."

"Yes," she said defiantly, "I did."

Bridget stared at her in disbelief. "But you were so kind, nursing me when I was ill—"

"You said Jack killed Mrs. Conway. You said you could identify him. I believed you were deliberately lying. But when you nearly died the other night, I realized you had been telling the truth—at least what you believed to be the truth. And I was sorry then I'd tried to discredit you."

"If Reston is innocent," Mike said, "it defeats me to explain why he didn't come forward and say so."

"Because all the evidence is against him," Peg said.

"Let's take it from the beginning," Mike said. When Peg remained silent, twisting her hands together in an agony of uncertainty, "Or would you rather tell the police?"

"We're in a bind," Reston said. "We should have

faced it in the first place. But I believe this guy is a straight shooter, Peg."

"Soft soap gathers no moss," Mike warned him.

"All right," Peg capitulated, "here goes. The truth, the whole truth, and nothing but the truth. But if you misuse it, Mike Graves, I'll—I'll—"

"Kill me with your bare hands," he prompted her. "Do sit down. I'm tired of standing."

She sat down on the bench between Mike and the big Jack Reston. "My name is Simone Marguerite Daumier, and I was the niece of Mrs. Conway's husband. He may have been justified about my father. I don't know because I never saw my father. He walked out when I was very young and left us penniless and my mother was sick a lot and she couldn't get any proper care. I never deliberately changed my name. My mother, after her marriage went on the rocks, dropped the Marguerite, and called me Margaret and then I became Peg. I hated my uncle and I hated his wife. We needed so little and it would have meant nothing to them. And then my uncle died and his wife became known as the great patroness of music students. That really hurt because I wanted to study music and I couldn't afford the lessons. I had a one-year scholarship in Germany but when that was over there wasn't a thing. A friend suggested that I apply to Mrs. Conway for assistance and I said I'd rather die. I told her that she was my aunt and she had never raised a finger to help me or my mother. I didn't want any Conway charity now.

"Well, my friend wrote to her without my knowledge and Mrs. Conway was awfully upset. She hadn't known about us at all. She replied, asking my friend to have me get in touch with her at once. She—I didn't know about the will. I never heard of it until the story came out after her death. Jack—we'd just been married three months—said it was time for me to stop being bitter. Mrs. Conway had suggested that I call on her any Saturday afternoon. I had a dentist appointment, of all things; so Jack said he would go to see her and heal the breach if he could, but, if she was disagreeable or patronizing, we'd just forget her.

"Well," Peg moistened her lips, "Jack went and rang the bell and no one answered. Then he noticed the door was ajar. He opened it partway and called. No one answered and there wasn't a sound inside. So he decided that no one was home, and he was coming away when he saw Bridget. And he never went inside. He never saw Mrs. Conway. He never knew until the story came out that she had been murdered. Never. Never!"

Bridget pushed her hair back from her face, bewildered.

"Bridget?"

"I don't know, Mike. It could have been that way. I suppose it could have been that way. I just thought—"

"But why didn't you come out with this story in the first place instead of going in for all these highjinks?" Mike demanded.

"Because," Reston put in, "we were caught flat-footed. What happens? We go out of town and miss the first account of Mrs. Conway's death. Next thing we know there is a big splash. Miss Evans has discovered Mrs. Conway's murdered body. She has seen me—and it was a good description—leaving the penthouse. And how could I explain my presence? I was calling on behalf of my wife, who was Mr. Conway's niece, who had hated Mrs. Conway's guts for years, and who was down for fifty thousand dollars in the will. What chance did we have?"

"Well, I—"

"Peg persuaded me to get out of town and come down here. You've found out that Jean is my sister? Well, she is."

"Oh, that's who she reminded me of," Bridget said. "She looks like you."

"We called the Lathams from New York and told them the whole story, and I've been holed up on a big ranch of Keith's practically ever since. And Peg—"

"I moved into Ma Baccante's to find out why Bridget was lying—as I thought—about Jack."

"And tried to discredit her," Mike said.

"I couldn't see any other way to discount her evidence against him. And then when she talked of leaving New York, I—"

"Walk into my parlor."

"Why not?" Peg was angry. "Jean and Keith played along because they knew Jack would never have injured anyone."

"And when did you begin to see the light?" Mike asked, his expression pleasant, his voice rough with anger.

"When someone tried to kill Bridget the other night. Then I knew I'd been all wrong. And I didn't know what to do."

"Are you willing to tell this whole story to the police?"

Reston laughed without amusement. "That's a rhetorical question, isn't it? I hate like hell to do it, but it's you or me. So let's go."

"Well?" Mike asked Bridget as they strolled toward the Gold Nugget to join the rest of the party for lunch.

"I don't know. I was so sure. I never doubted for a moment that he was the one who killed Liz."

"And now?"

"I believe he is telling the truth. I believe they are both telling the truth."

"And now?"

"And now we are left with Frank and Oliver, and I can't believe for a moment that either of them had anything to do with Liz or that either of them would hurt me."

Mike grunted. "At least we've cleared up my doubts about Peg. I never trusted her for a moment; the whole deal stank. It was obvious from the beginning that she must be the one to plant that hypodermic in your room. Now I can concentrate on something else. With the large young man identified and—we hope—eliminated as a suspect—" He broke off as they entered the restaurant.

"You're not sure about him, are you?" Bridget said in a low tone and preceded him toward the table where Keith had stood up to signal them.

16

"It occurs to me," Mike said, while he was acting as bartender before dinner, "now the cards are down there is no particular point in us keeping up the pretense of being paying guests."

"I wish you'd stay," Jean said. "Bridget needs the sun and, anyhow, I guess we all owe it to her. And Keith and I would honestly like it."

"It's not that easy, you know," Mike told her. "We can't keep Jack Reston's identity from the police. It alters the whole shape of the case."

"Oh, no!" Peg protested.

"Oh, yes," Reston agreed. "Anyhow, I can't remain in hiding any longer. This can't go on."

"No, it can't go on," Mike said.

"Then we're just going to bust up?" Oliver said blankly. "I for one am going to hate that. I know I don't really belong to this party but I've enjoyed it a lot. I had hoped we could do a bit more sight-seeing together —at least see Sedona and the cliff dwellings."

"I'd like that too," Frank said, "before we just go our separate ways."

Mike looked at his watch. "With the time difference I couldn't reach Lieutenant Baxter tonight, and he's the only one I know personally on the force. Tomor-

row I'll tell him who Jack is and say he can stop looking for Bridget's large young man." There was an
odd expression on his face.

"Oh," Bridget said, "I hadn't realized. If Jack Reston
is eliminated, I'm back as the chief suspect in Liz's
murder." She set down her glass with a shaking hand
and then picked it up again, afraid to leave it unat-
tended on the table. She wondered whether she could
ever again be free of fear—fear of herself, fear of other
people, fear of life.

After dinner Frank cornered her and talked about
his opera until she yawned widely and was sorry when
he flushed.

"I didn't mean to bore you," he said stiffly and went
away.

In her own room Bridget turned the key in the
lock and went to put a chair against the French window. It had a shiny new lock. So that was what Mike
had been doing after dinner. That meant, didn't it,
that he knew she was still in danger.

It was nearly morning before she slept. In Peg's
room a low-voiced conversation went on hour after
hour. Reston could be innocent, Bridget assured herself.
He could be telling the truth. Perhaps he never had
gone inside the penthouse. But who had left the door
ajar? If Reston was not the murderer, who had preceded him?

She slept at last and seemed only to have fallen
asleep when there was a tap at the door, and Keith
called, "Arise and shine! We're going to Sedona to see
Oak Creek Canyon and, believe me, it's worth it. Jean is
making waffles. Come and git it before she throws it in
the crick."

Bridget tumbled out of bed, half asleep, and showered and dressed quickly. This morning Peg's face was glowing, almost pretty, and radiant when she looked at her husband.

Oliver was excited. "I wish—do any of you have field glasses? I'd like to get a good view of this place. I've been interested in cliff dwellings all my life."

"I have glasses," Keith said.

"If you'll excuse me." Mike went into the living room and closed the door.

"He is going to call the New York police about you," Peg told her husband.

"Okay, dearest. It has to be done."

"And then what will happen?" Jean asked.

"Then," Reston said levelly, "our pretty Bridget is going to have to eat some of her words."

"Leave us have no bullying," Oliver said. He put his hand over Bridget's. "There's not a drop of vindictive blood in this girl's veins. If you had the brains of a louse, you'd know that."

"You coming along on this safari?" Keith asked his wife.

"I'll have to do something about dinner."

"We can go to Neptune's Table and have fish." Keith laughed. "That's what I like about modern civilization. Fresh fish daily in the desert. The cliff dwellers didn't have it so good."

They heard a loud exclamation from Mike, heard him say, "Are you sure? . . . Well, I'll be eternally damned."

There was a queer expression on his face when he came back into the room. He shook his head at Jean's offer of another waffle, ignored the curious eyes that watched for a clue to what he had just learned.

"Let's go," Keith said.

"I'll take Peg," Reston said, "if it's all right to go on using your Volvo."

"Oh, sure. Go ahead. When you get to Sedona, park anywhere on the main street and we'll find you. Or if we get separated we can meet for lunch at the Turtle."

"Don't get any ideas and try to get away," Mike warned Reston. "The police have long arms."

"Damn it, we're not—"

"And when do we visit the cliff dwellings?" Oliver asked hastily.

"On our way back. And if you want to take color pictures of the canyon, you'll find it worth doing. The colors are something. Often as I've seen them they really stop my breath every time."

"No camera, unfortunately. How about you?"

For once Frank and Oliver vied for Bridget's attention in a good humor, without friction or hostility. Bridget found herself enjoying the ride. It was Keith who first broached the subject of the telephone call which loomed so large in all their minds. "Did you get your man in New York?"

"Oh, yes, thanks."

"What is he going—can you tell us how this will affect Jack? How he stands? He's a good Joe, Mike, a really good Joe. I'm not saying that simply because he is my brother-in-law. I've known him a long time, longer than I have Jean, as a matter of fact, and he's as straight as they come. He just stumbled into this damned spot, and I guess we all blundered about the best way to extricate him."

II

As the saguaros thinned and finally disappeared from the desert face, there were low hills in the distance. Gradually, as they approached, the hills took on faint streaks of pink and rose. Then a turn in the road brought cries from the Lathams' paying guests. Ahead were red cliffs, a flaming brilliant red, built in fantastic shapes, looking like gigantic modern sculptures. And always above was the deep brilliant blue of the sky.

"It's too much," Bridget said. "That first day when I lay in the sun and looked at the pool and the blue sky and the desert plants and the tropical trees and bushes and listened to a mockingbird I thought it was like an extravagant stage set, but this—no man could ever have conceived of this."

"How would you like to live here always, sweetie?" Oliver asked. "That's my dream. But it wouldn't be much without you." Before she could speak he said, "Think of it, anyhow."

Frank, who had been adjusting the glasses Keith had lent him, handed them to Bridget. "It's fantastically beautiful, isn't it?"

When she had studied the brilliant rock structure she passed on the glasses to Oliver.

"There's your Volvo," Jean told her husband.

"Want to stop now?"

"No, let's go on to where the road begins to switch back and you lose the brilliance of the canyon in the trees. Then we can come back here and meet them at the Turtle."

They were all silent when they had found a turning space, and started back down the canyon. Oliver put his hand lightly on Bridget's. "Good lord, you're catching cold! Your hand is like ice."

"No, I'm just so—excited. Too excited for words. It's so much more beauty than I can bear." Her voice shook.

"What you need," Mike said practically, "is a drink."

"It's too hot for a cocktail."

"A rum collins, just slightly tart and very, very cold."

And it was over tall glasses of rum collins that they met Peg and Jack Reston, who had taken a large table and were waiting for them, cocktails in front of them.

For a little while the talk was casual, once the important matter of ordering the lunch was taken care of. Frank and Oliver discussed the canyon. Oliver laughingly accused Keith Latham of taking a kind of proprietary interest as though he had invented the thing or at least owned it.

Peg said suddenly, "Bridget, do you have any dark glasses?"

She shook her head.

"Jack, will you get some? There's bound to be a drugstore in town. You'll need them, Bridget. You can't imagine how blinding those chalky cliffs can be under a brilliant sun."

"I thought you hadn't been in Arizona before."

"Oh, well." Peg dismissed her lies airily. "Actually we spent our honeymoon on Keith's ranch. Oh, and another thing. Watch your step on the path up to Montezuma's Castle. Those lime cliffs can crumble. And when it's hot the rattlesnakes come out."

"Ugh."

"At least," Bridget remarked to Frank, who had remained tenaciously beside her from the time they approached Montezuma's Castle, "you can't say they didn't warn us."

She pointed to a glass case which displayed the particular horrors to watch out for on the path to the cliff dwelling: rattlesnakes, Gila monsters, scorpions, black widow spiders. She shivered. Frank's warm hand was comforting on flesh that was chilled with horror and disgust.

As they walked along the narrow path that led to the cliff dwelling, Bridget was grateful for the sunglasses Jack Reston had procured for her in Sedona. The sun beat relentlessly on her head; the glare of the sun on the incredibly high white cliff was blinding.

"And this," Oliver said, looking up from a pamphlet, "is the way the Indians lived in the twelfth century. They lived in those caves in the cliff you can see up there, with ladders to the ground and passages between their various rooms, or whatever they were, in the rock."

"Think of the heat and the smells and the smoke. Even an animal lives better than that," Bridget said. "I thought it would be more romantic."

"Romantic!" Frank laughed.

"Well, the noble Redskin. Nature's nobleman. All that. No one seeing this could be too tough on our contemporary civilization."

"Hey, you stop running down my cliff dwelling," Keith said in mock indignation. "All right. Who's going up? Just an easy stroll. You're only allowed to go to the top of the path. Beyond that the cliff crumbles and the ceilings of the dwellings inside have fallen."

He started at a brisk pace, followed by Jean and Peg. Bridget walked with Frank while Oliver was close behind with Mike and Reston.

The path, as Keith had said, was an easy stroll, if the walker kept an eye out for loose gravel and whatever might have crawled out from under a rock.

"I wish we could go inside," Oliver said. "I'd like to know more about the way they actually lived and managed."

"Well, you can't," Keith assured him. "The whole thing could crash in on you."

"Look, here's a cave. Let me have your glasses, Keith."

Keith handed them over. "Nothing to see in there," he said impatiently and started down the far path that led to the ground.

Oliver stooped to enter the great cave, whose roof sloped steeply down at the back. He crawled forward until he could look into a smaller cave beyond. "Good God! There's someone in there."

"Can't be," Reston said as he crawled in beside him.

"But there is. It looks like a body."

"But it can't—give me those glasses. Looks more like a bundle of rags. I wish I had a flashlight."

"Here." Frank took out a match strip, held it carefully and lighted a match, then set them all off and tossed the blazing strip into the cloth in the inner cave.

Bridget, made uneasy by being too close to Reston, crawled out. For a moment she blinked, blinded by the dazzling sun because she had removed her dark glasses in the cave, and then she felt the hard blow on her shoulder. Her feet slipped from under her and she was falling.

III

Oliver was crying. That was the improbable thing. He was kneeling beside her, his face as white as the cliff that loomed precipitously behind him, and he was crying. She tried to reassure him.

"I'm all right."

"Sure, she's all right." That was Mike's voice. "One thing I've learned. As long as this gal falls on her head, she is safe."

"Why you—" she began indignantly, and then she saw that Mike was sitting beside her, propped against the cliff, his face unnaturally pale, his left arm in a sling that was made of the green scarf Peg had worn over her hair. "What happened to you?"

"Apparently a broken arm. Nothing that won't heal." He managed a smile. "If I've survived Peg's treatment I can survive anything."

"I'm terribly sorry," Peg said. "I tried not to hurt you."

"What happened?" Bridget asked.

There was a confused babble of voices. It was Oliver who said, "I heard you scream and I came a-running. You were going over the cliff headfirst and so was Mike. About all I could do was to grab the cuffs of your slacks and at least break the fall a bit, but Mike landed on his left elbow." Oliver became aware of his tears and brushed them away in embarrassment. "I guess I must really love you," he said in a tone of wonder, and Bridget saw Mike watching him, a queer twist to his lips.

Bridget looked around. Jean was watching her somberly. Peg, the freckles prominent on her face, was looking at her husband.

Reston bent over Bridget who involuntarily shrank back. Her movement brought a hard light to his eyes. A short distance away the usual throng of sight-seers had gathered, staring at them, and being herded on by an attendant.

Men came with a stretcher, which both Bridget and Mike refused, and then they were escorted to an ambulance, after one of the interns rolled up Mike's sleeve and gave him a shot.

Neither of them spoke until they had nearly reached Phoenix, riding through the Black Canyon with its dark hills and trees. "As though we were really going down into an inferno," Mike said, and his voice startled her.

"Poor Mike."

"I'm okay."

"I didn't slip, you know. I was pushed." Bridget asked anxiously, "Do you believe me?"

He reached for her with his sound hand. "I believe you. I was pushed too."

"It was Reston, wasn't it?"

He grinned at her. The needle had begun to take effect and he was not quite so alarmingly pale. "There's an old S.S. Van Dine mystery novel I read once and never forgot. The detective was supposed to be the hell of a clever guy but he suspected everyone in turn until, one by one, they were picked off by the murderer. When there was only one left even he could figure it out."

"I don't see the point."

"Don't you?"

"Don't be infuriating. How much more of this do you think I can take?"

"You won't have to take anything more."

"You know who's behind this?"

"Yes, but I can't prove it. Not yet. I have to make a telephone call first."

"Someone pushed us. If it wasn't Reston—and Oliver saved my life. Mike, why was he crying? He doesn't care all that much about me."

"Perhaps he does," Mike said gently. "He was crying because that bunch of burning matches Frank tossed into the inner cave set fire to a bundle of old rags in which I am prepared to bet a year's pay Oliver had hidden eighty thousand dollars. Hadn't you guessed, Bridget? He's the Phoenix Wizard, just released from the pen. Baxter told me over the phone after I'd sent on fingerprints."

"Fingerprints!"

"The plastic coaster. He had to be up to something. And there was the story of the Phoenix Wizard and the prison pallor and the generally convincing charm of the good con man, and he was so hell-bent on coming to Montezuma's Castle. He could have gone alone, of course, but there was always a chance he'd be remembered. In a crowd he was less likely to be noticed. Anyhow, I imagine what he chiefly wanted was to assure himself the loot was still there. He must have spent a year thinking about it."

"Oliver a thief! I can't believe it. And he let it burn up to save me. Poor Oliver."

"Where—oh, this must be the hospital. Keep your chin up, Bridget. They'll probably x-ray that thick skull of yours and set my arm properly and send us home. It's nearly over, you know."

17

"I wish," Mike said irritably, for the setting of his arm had not been a pleasant affair, "that our tireless murderer would not stage his efforts at a time when I can't reach Lieutenant Baxter. That time difference queers the works. But at least I can count on my dear old mother for help."

He got change and shut himself awkwardly in a telephone booth. When he came out he was smiling. "She's going to give us a hand. You'll like her, Bridget. Oh, and that reminds me, she told me to be sure to bring you to her when we get back to New York."

"But, Mike, that's impossible."

"Why is it?"

She countered with a question of her own. "What happens next?"

"We just have to get through tonight."

"All right," Bridget agreed reluctantly. "Anyhow, Jack Reston wouldn't dare do anything at the Latham house. He may be Jean's brother, but they wouldn't stand for that. You know, Mike, at this point I'm so tired I just don't care. And so sorry about Oliver. Maybe he's a crook and a thief but I'm honestly sorry about the money. He lost it to save me. I end by hurting everyone, don't I?"

"Well, you two wrecks! I must say you don't do

credit to the Latham hospitality." Keith came across the lobby of the hospital, grinning at them and shaking his head. "How bad is it?"

"One broken arm and one bumped head," Mike said laconically. "The verdict seems to be that we'll live."

Keith eased Bridget into the back seat of the Cadillac. "Jean sent a pillow so you can lie down if you like." He watched while Mike got awkwardly into the front seat and slammed the door behind him.

Mike tried to turn around to look at Bridget but was thwarted by the cast.

"She's lying down," Keith said, his voice low.

"Did you find them?"

Keith grinned. "The purloined letter."

"You mean they were right in sight? I thought I had searched every inch of your house at one time and another."

"On the dresser in a neat stack of boxes of film."

"Film! But why—"

"Well," and Keith chuckled, "I remembered no one had a camera."

"Oh, my God!" Mike said in disgust. "What a detective I turned out to be. It's a good thing this case is closed."

"Is it?"

"It will be in the morning. By the way, would it surprise you to know that Oliver Putnam is the Phoenix Wizard, and his cache was in that bundle of rags in the inner cave where, I suppose, it could have lain forever until he could reclaim it."

"Oliver! And the whole thing went in in flames before his eyes." After a long time Keith said, "You know something? Oliver is a good guy. He could have put out that fire and instead he hurled himself half off the cliff to hang onto Bridget." At a stop light, he turned to look at her. "I think she's asleep."

"Good. She's just about had it."

"What do we do now, Mike?"

"Mark time and wait for instructions from New York in the morning. They will probably call in the Phoenix police to make the arrest. It may be unpleasant. Perhaps you had better get the girls out of the house first. Take them shopping or sight-seeing or something. Jean can think up some excuse to get them away."

"And leave you alone to handle this thing with a broken arm and not so much as a gun?"

"Reston strikes me as a good guy to have on your side in a fight—if it comes to a fight."

"He is. None better. I'm glad you think so. This whole setup has placed him in a bad light, and I must say it's been against his wishes all along. He wanted to march into police headquarters and say he was Bridget's large young man and explain what had happened. But when you consider Bridget was positive, as an eye witness, that he had been inside and he was married to Mr. Conway's niece who had inherited fifty thousand dollars and there was that damning phrase about 'old grudges,' it just didn't seem as though he had a chance of being believed. Talk about the cards being stacked! Peg got on the phone with us and we suggested that Jack come out here and stay on the ranch until the heat was off, while Peg sized up Bridget to figure out why she had lied about Jack. Well, you know all about that now. I hope this new development will clear him completely. What do you think?"

"Considering that two attempts have been made to kill Bridget, the sleeping pills followed by that shove off Montezuma's Castle this afternoon, and you've found the sleeping pills, all we need now is a clear identification. It's always possible to say that the sleeping pills were planted, but an identification also provides motive, which has been the tricky point from the beginning."

"I think I can figure out everything now except you. What got you into this, Mike?"

"I told Bridget it was my mother. In a sense that is true." Mike explained about Field's deep attachment to his dead client and his eagerness to know the truth about Bridget Evans, who was in a equivocal position. "I had some free time—I write television plays and I was well ahead of schedule—"

"You're that Michael Graves! Good God! I had no idea. You don't get out of Phoenix until the Lathams have had a chance to exploit you. Our only celebrity."

"Don't be an ass! Anyhow, my mother said, 'Why don't you take a look at the girl?' And—"

"And all Graves needed was one look and—"

"Go to hell!"

Keith laughed and drew up at the house. He went around to open the door. "Make it all right?"

"Sure." Mike got out, wincing as he knocked his left arm against the door. "Damn! I'm off balance. How about Bridget?"

"Old iron-woman Bridget. She'll make it on her own two feet. Come on, honey." He opened the door and leaned in to shake the sleeping girl by the shoulder.

Bridget sat up with a start, her heart pounding.

"Oh, what a fool I am. I didn't mean to scare you. It's all right. We're home. Hey, Mike."

"Yes?" Mike turned at something urgent in Keith's voice.

"What do we do about Oliver?"

"In a showdown he let that loot go to save Bridget.

How many people do you know of whom you could say as much?"

"Not many. And he had a year in prison."

"Let's welcome him back to the human race. I know a lot of better guys I don't like half as well."

II

Mike had passed a restless night. His arm was painful, he could not lie in any comfortable position because of the cast, and, though he tried to think clearly, his thoughts were in a jumble. Suppose he had been mistaken all along? Suppose Baxter's information and what he might be able to tell him conflicted with the theory he had built up. Suppose at the time of the confrontation there should be violence in some form for which he was unprepared. Suppose—

He tried to turn, was blocked by the cast, and cursed silently to himself. On the lounge next to him, outside Bridget's window, Keith was snoring peacefully. Behind Peg's window a light burned. From Oliver's open window drifted the scent of tobacco and now and then a red glow showed for a moment. Oliver too was sleepless. Poor Oliver who had risked so much and paid so dearly for a fortune and who had lost it by a moment's instinctive gesture to save a human life. This must be a bitter night for him. The end of a long dream, the fading of the plans he had made, the facing of an empty future.

Frank's room was quiet. Once he had been assured that neither Bridget nor Mike had been seriously injured and that Bridget would be carefully guarded all night, he had taken himself off to his room with a book.

Mike drifted into sleep and was awakened first by an awareness of the chill of the early morning and again when he felt someone hovering near him and opened his eyes to see Jean putting a second blanket on her husband's lounge. Then she came quietly to pull another blanket over him. He was asleep again before he could thank her.

He was awakened by Keith saying in a low voice, "Mike! Mike!" He tried to get up in a hurry and remembered the cast.

"What is it?" It was still dark. Surely nothing else had happened. "Nearly seven o'clock. Nine o'clock in New York. You wanted me to call you early."

"Oh, thanks a lot."

Keith held out his arm, braced himself, and Mike hauled himself up, grunting.

"I'll help you with shoes and things. Don't bother with a shower."

When Mike came out of his room, a sweater slung over his shoulders, his face rather unevenly shaved, he went straight to the telephone. Keith brought him a cup of steaming coffee. "Want me to dial?" When he had got the number, he handed the phone to Mike, nodded, and went out, closing the door behind him.

"Mother? . . . Oh, the arm is fine. Did you learn anything?" He listened for a long time. At last he drew a long breath. "You're a living wonder. That's the thing that had me baffled all the time. . . . No, but it will be over today. . . . I'll bring her if she'll come with me. . . . I'm sure about myself but not about her. She's had a lot of strikes against her and she's not sure—not about me, not about herself, not about anything. . . . Bless you."

Mike signaled for Keith to dial a second number. "Lieutenant Baxter? This is Michael Graves. . . . I really slipped up this time. . . . No, just a broken arm. Miss Evans got a scalp wound and some assorted scrapes and bruises. She would have had a broken hip or back—or her neck—if it hadn't been for Oliver Putnam. . . . I know, it's a fantastic story, isn't it? . . . What did you find, Lieutenant? . . . No question about the identification? . . . Oh, sure it fits. It fits perfectly. I got some corroboration this morning of a different kind from my mother. Tell you more when I see you in New York. And, incidentally, we've got the sleeping pills. Must be at least a hundred of them . . . No, we can't let it linger on . . . Yes, I'll swear to it if necessary . . . You'll call the Phoenix police and brief them thoroughly. Our least favorite character is damnably plausible. If it hadn't been for one palpable lie right at the beginning, I'd have been completely taken in. . . . What's that? They've already been alerted? Oh, good . . . Bring Miss Evans back to New York? . . . Well, that depends on her, doesn't it? . . . Mr. Field says—what! What the hell does he think I am? Casanova?" Mike heard the lieutenant laugh, joined in reluctantly, and put down the telephone.

Jean, a robe over her nightgown, was preparing breakfast while Keith was setting the table.

"Good lord," Mike protested, "I didn't expect you to go to all this trouble. The coffee was fine but—at this hour—"

"There isn't much time, is there?" Jean said soberly. "Things are going to happen now, aren't they?"

"They are going to end," Mike said reassuringly.

"But first—they happen. Just what, Mike?"

"You know now, don't you?"

"Well, Keith told me about your guess and then he found the sleeping pills, but it seems so unlikely. Were you right?"

"According to Lieutenant Baxter. He got a perfect description that fits like a glove, and I've got corroboration of another kind."

"So?"

"So we'll have the police here this morning prepared to make an arrest. Baxter is arranging it from the New York end."

"Then I'd better get dressed. Keith, you watch the bacon and keep turning it with the tongs. And the cantaloupe is cut and ready to serve. You can put on the plates and—"

"Off with you and get into a dress. Somehow blue jeans don't strike quite the right note for an arrest."

"Don't joke. It's not funny."

Mike sat at the kitchen table sipping coffee, while Keith put cantaloupe at each place at the dining room table and turned bacon.

"What about the others?" Mike asked.

"Jean says it's going to be bad enough when the time comes. She wants them to sleep as long as they can."

Jean came back, wearing a dark blue linen dress, her hair fastened in a loose knot on her head, and took over the tongs while Keith made toast. Then she broke eggs into a dish and turned as Jack Reston, all six-foot-three of him, came into the kitchen.

He looked from one face to another. "Do you people know what time it is, for God's sake? Seven-thirty. What worm are you early birds trying to catch?" Something in the silence that followed his unfortunate words made him say quickly, "Has anything more happened?"

"The police are going to get here any minute now," Jean said somberly. "Eat your cantaloupe, and I'll scramble some eggs."

Reston's eyes met Mike's with a challenge in them.

"And who are the police coming to see?"

"Is something wrong?" Oliver stood in the doorway, dressed with his usual meticulous care. He had never seemed better looking. Some of the prison pallor had been replaced by a golden tan. But his mouth was colorless and his eyes were sunken from looking too long into a bleak future.

"The Phoenix police are on their way," Mike said.

"Oh?" Oliver sat down rather heavily on the kitchen chair next to Mike's, and lighted a cigarette with shaking fingers. "Oh? Old friends of mine, I believe."

Keith shoved a cup of coffee toward him. Oliver forced a smile. "The last meal of the condemned?"

"Don't be a fool, Oliver," Keith said. "We know about you. The police have nothing on you. You served your time and you're a free man. It's not you they are after."

"Who then?"

"Frank Snodgrass, alias Frank Saunders."

Peg came into the kitchen. "Where in the world is Bridget? I knocked on her door and then went in. She isn't there and she isn't on the terrace. I don't—"

Mike lurched to his feet and was running. They heard him knock on a door, then bang on it. He shouted, "Frank!"

He turned to look at the frightened faces. "He's got her. He must have guessed when he found the sleeping pills were gone. He's got Bridget!"

There was a ring at the door bell and Keith went to open it. "Police," a pleasant voice said. "Are you Keith Latham?"

"Come in," Keith said. "But you're too late. He's gone and he's taken the girl with him."

18

Bridget tried to fix her hair, but, after the first painful stroke of her hairbrush, she did not attempt to do anything with the soft dusky hair that waved close to her head. She explored the sore lump, saw the black and blue swelling on her thigh and the skinned patch of her skin which had bled so profusely and which had been neatly bandaged at the hospital. She put on slacks and a sweater, feeling like a pincushion.

Lie in the sun. She was shaken by unexpected laughter that was close to tears. *I get doped and pushed and—*

But it was over. Mike had said so. Today the police would come for Reston. She felt a pang for Peg and then remembered Liz Conway with the noose embedded in her throat.

She looked at her watch. Seven-thirty. She was too wide awake to attempt to sleep, and it would be some time before breakfast would be ready. Vacationers like to sleep late. She looked out on the terrace, saw that it was deserted, and stepped out, glad of the warmth of her sweater in the early morning coolness. Then Frank's window opened and he came out, shaping a "good morning" with his lips. She waved to him.

"You couldn't sleep either?" he asked in a whisper.

She shook her head and then clutched it with both hands. "Ouch!"

"We can't talk like this. We'll just wake everyone up. Let's get out for a bit, shall we? The air's so fresh this time of the morning."

"I'm not sure I can walk far," Bridget said. "I'm wobbly."

"Heavens, no. I wouldn't expect you to. We can take Latham's car. He won't be using it at this time of day. I'll get the key. He keeps it hanging on the nail inside the door."

He came back with the key and she followed him out. The car was where Keith had left it when he brought Bridget and Mike back to the house. Frank helped Bridget in, whispered, "Don't slam the door yet or you'll wake them," and let off the brake. The car coasted down the road, he started the motor, and then they slammed the doors and were off.

"What did Mike tell you last night?" Frank asked suddenly.

"Nothing except that he was going to call the police in New York this morning."

"In New York!" Frank exclaimed in amazement. "Oh, I suppose they can get Reston sent back there without trouble. That was quite a shock when he turned out to be Peg's husband. That really shook me. And all the time she was protecting him and trying to involve you. That was a pretty lousy trick, Bridget."

"Well, of course—"

"Quite an actress Peg turned out to be, shielding a guy like that. You'd think she'd be afraid of him when she remembers how he stood behind her aunt and dropped that noose over her head and watched her hands trying to drag it away, watched them fall at last and—"

"Frank!"

"Hm?"

"Let's go back."

"What's the hurry? They're all asleep."

"I want to go back now, Frank. Now!"

He turned his head for a swift look. "No, Bridget. You aren't going back. We're neither of us going back."

"Why?"

"They found the sleeping pills last night. I knew then. I always knew you'd destroy me."

"It was you, Frank? Why?"

"I guess you could call me nemesis," he said, "or retribution. You killed my sister Louisa as surely as though you had put a bullet into her brain. You destroyed her chance of becoming a great singer. You persuaded Mrs. Conway to give you the help and the money that belonged to Louisa. So Louisa died, young and pretty and hopeful until you ended her chances and destroyed her hope. Between you two women she was destroyed. Mrs. Conway knew she was to blame because she offered to pay for Louisa's funeral!" He choked. "Her funeral!" His voice rose. "When it should have been her hour of success, with people clapping and shouting and Louisa smiling and bowing and waving as I've seen her do a hundred times before her mirror when she was planning for it. And I knew you were guilty too. You told me yourself you'd do anything to be able to sing."

For a moment Bridget was aware only of the sickness she had felt when she saw Louisa Snodgrass run stumbling out of Liz Conway's music room, when she had read the account of her suicide blamed on Bridget Evans.

"Frank," she said humbly, "I'm more sorry than I can say. I didn't mean it. I didn't do anything to influence Liz. That's as true as that I live. It was bad enough to know she blamed me and to feel so terribly —terribly sorry for her—but if I had never existed, the result would have been the same. Please try to believe me, Frank. Your sister couldn't really sing. She just thought she could. She was unbalanced, you know."

"That's a contemptible lie. She was as sane as I am."

"It's the truth. She had no voice at all. Mr. Field, Mrs. Conway's lawyer, checked up on her at the time of her suicide. She had—imagined things before, thought people were against her. She—like your mother—" The words faded out.

The big powerful car put on a burst of speed. The highway was practically deserted. The eastbound road was a quarter of a mile away. The speedometer leaped from sixty to seventy to eighty. When Bridget raised her eyes from the speedometer to Frank's face she saw the tightly compressed lips, the fanatically gleaming eyes; she then went back to the speedometer. Ninety, a hundred, a hundred and ten—the car rocked as he changed lanes, and Bridget closed her eyes.

There was no one to call. She couldn't jump. Frank. It had been Frank all the time. She had to keep her mind on Frank, to think about him. Otherwise terror would take possession of her, and if she had any chance at all, it would be because she held on to her control, kept her mind functioning. As long as she refused to panic there was a chance.

She couldn't reach Frank. He would never believe that she was not responsible for his sister's suicide. How had she been so blind? She had accepted him at his face value, a little amused by his obsession with his opera, touched by his apparent devotion to her. And it had all been a lie. Frank—gentle and unobtrusive and shy. Frank who had strangled Liz Conway and planned to destroy her.

He might kill her. He would probably kill her, but he could not escape. She took a quick look at him, wondering what distorted thoughts were in his mind. Escape for himself did not matter to him. He had gone beyond that, beyond any weighing of chances, beyond any fear for his own safety.

As though echoing her own thoughts he said, "I have to do it for Louisa. That's what she wants. Someone must pay for all her lovely dreams that turned to ashes. And then I'll be through." He gave her his shy boyish smile. "You know," he confided naïvely, "I'm glad it's nearly over. I'm so tired. I haven't slept soundly a single night since Louisa died. And when I do sleep—the nightmares! I'll be glad to get a good night's sleep again."

They had left the saguaros behind, and the hills were looming up dimly ahead as light came back to the sky. Where on earth were they going? Then she knew. Back to Montezuma's Castle. But he couldn't possibly expect her to climb that path of her own free will, and he was not powerful enough to carry her. It was a crazy idea. Crazy. Of course.

She swayed and lurched against the safety belt as the car rocketed down the road. She was afraid to look at the speedometer. Perhaps, she thought with a ray of hope, they would run out of gas. But she recalled that Keith had stopped to fill the tank on their way back from the hospital the night before.

Keith would discover that his car was missing and call the police. She managed to steady herself enough to look at her watch. Eighty-thirty. At this speed they would be reaching the cliff dwelling before long. Yes, there was the sign and the arrow pointing to Montezuma's Castle. They were on the long narrow road that led steeply downhill. A helicopter buzzed overhead.

There was a fine perspiration on Frank's face though the morning was cool. You could possibly touch a chord of pity in a criminal mind, Bridget thought, but you couldn't reason with a mad mind.

"Frank, why did you kill Mrs. Conway?"

"I saw a picture of her in a Sunday paper, the music section, telling about her generosity to young singers. Generosity! I wanted to know what kind of woman she was. I discovered that my father had put away quite a bit of cash, seven or eight hundred dollars, so I stuck it in my pocket and went off one day to get a good look at you. But first I got those sleeping pills Louisa had been gathering for a long time. Well, Louisa had heard you and Mrs. Conway talking about the Baccante place, so I got a room there where I could see you for myself. I said I was a composer. I had to be something and I couldn't play any instrument and there was a lodger where we lived who used to encourage Louisa and talked to her by the hour about an opera he was writing that had a big part for her. I remembered what he said. It was a relevant theme and the music was part conventional and part mod. I remembered all of it."

Bridget gave a gasp. "Of course! That's what Mike saw in the beginning, but I suppose we were all so used to the racket we never gave it a thought. Mike realized no one would attempt to compose music with that uproar going on around him."

"So Mike knows. He fell for you too, of course. Mike and Oliver and me. God help me, I fell in love with you! It was treachery to Louisa, but I couldn't help it. So I didn't know what to do. Here you were sitting on top of the world, taking lessons from the great Madame Woolf, being helped by Mrs. Conway. And yet I couldn't bear to hurt you. You were so—so sweet. I nearly gave up the whole idea. I thought maybe I'd marry you. I let days and weeks go by because I couldn't make up my mind. And at night I'd dream of Louisa. She'd come to ask me what I was waiting for. So I went to see Mrs. Conway."

"You intended to kill her?"

"I made a little noose. It was surprisingly easy. You have no idea how easy it is to kill someone, Bridget," he said casually, "if you really plan it. Anyhow, I was justified in what I was doing so luck was on my side. The lobby of the building was empty. Not a soul saw me. I took the elevator and rang the bell. Mrs. Conway called, 'Who is it?' I called back, 'Bridget gave me a message for you.' "

"Oh, no," Bridget cried in protest.

"It was only right, you see. After all, you were responsible. So she opened the door. She had been looking over some scores in the music room and she took me in there and sat down and offered me a seat. And I stepped behind her to look at a signed photograph on the wall and dropped the noose over her head. It was very quick, though I held on quite a time to make sure that she was dead. Then I just walked out and I guess I didn't pull the door shut behind me. I never worried about a thing. I knew it was foreordained to be all right. There was no one in the lobby. As I reached the street, I saw this big fellow turning into the building, who turned out to be your large young man. Jack Reston. What a laugh, Bridget.

"Because you walked in on the guy and thought he had killed her. And then you landed in the hospital. I had planned to give you the sleeping pills but when you came back, so sick and weak and so—so damned appealing—and someone was obviously gunning for you and you were mine—so I waited. And when you came west with Peg I came along. I knew I could get over loving you if I tried hard enough, and then I could go ahead and do what I had to do."

"So you doped the rum punch."

"That's when my luck changed. Because those people got themselves killed right outside the house and caused all that racket and Mike found you before you died."

The helicopter was overhead again. The parking lot, which had been filled the day before, was empty except for a single car, but there was no one in sight.

"Get out," Frank said, and his forehead gleamed with perspiration.

"No!"

He came around the car to open the door. "Get out!" He laughed. "Last stop." He reached in, released her safety belt, and jerked her out so that she fell on her knees. "Come on."

She turned, clawing at the car but there was nothing to hold on to. She screamed, knowing that no one could answer her. He dragged her to her feet.

I'm not going to help you kill me, she thought, and she refused to move so that he had to drag her, her toes digging into the path as he went around the building where tickets were sold and information provided. She was thankful for the slacks which, to some extent, protected her legs from the gravel path. She screamed again, calling nobody, calling because human beings must cry for help even when it is not forthcoming.

Then a number of things were happening at once. The helicopter was settling slowly on the ground. A car roared into the parking lot spilling out uniformed men, and the door of the museum opened and a man stood on the path in front of them, a gun in his hand.

Frank looked at him, looked at Bridget. "You have destroyed everything. Now you destroy me." Then he turned and dodged past the man who had blocked his way, running toward the path that led up the chalky lime of the cliff dwelling. The policeman bent over Bridget, helped her to her feet. "You all right?" When she nodded he turned and shouted, "Stop! Stop or I'll fire."

Frank halted for a moment and then he reached the turn in the path, started to claw his way straight up the surface of the great ancient structure.

The policeman fired a warning shot, far to the right, which chipped the surface. Frank was hauling himself up frantically. "Where the hell does he think he is going?" the policeman demanded of no one in particular. He fired again, this time carefully over Frank's head, and bits of chalk crumpled and fell into the upturned face.

Frank was close to the top now, nearly a hundred and fifty feet above the path. Half a dozen men had congregated from the helicopter and the car, several of them with drawn guns.

Frank was at the top, an arm hooked over the rim to support him. He turned his head, looked down at the watching men. His shoulder muscles bunched as he started to drag himself over the top and then he paused, waved his free hand at them, and deliberately released his hold. And then he was falling, turning over in the air, screaming thinly. There was a hideous sound, and the men, who had stood spellbound, were running forward, leaving Bridget alone on the path.

19

"Get in," Mike snapped and ducked his head toward the Cadillac. Keith, Jack Reston, and Oliver had scrambled out of the Volvo, and they waited while Mike went forward alone to Bridget.

"I'm taking her home," Mike called to the policemen. It was not a request.

"We'll see her later," one of them said. "We've got to get her story but it can wait."

"You'll get it." Mike's good hand was on the door of the Cadillac when Keith came running.

"Here, you can't drive with one arm. I'll take you back. The others can come in the Volvo." He looked anxiously at Bridget's gray face. "How bad is it?"

"She isn't hurt," Mike said. "But she saw Frank go." He got into the back seat beside her, cursing as he knocked the cast. "You little fool," he said furiously. "You damned little fool. Do you know how close you came to getting yourself killed?"

"I know," she said huskily. "But you came in time."

"Don't give me that. No credit to me you aren't lying smashed at the foot of that cliff. I was asleep at the switch. If Baxter hadn't been ahead of me all the time and alerted the Phoenix police, nothing could have saved you this morning."

"How did they find us?"

"They never lost you. They've had men on guard for several days. The one who wants to shoot himself is the one who followed us up to Montezuma's Castle yesterday and then got stuck with a bunch of tourists and saw you fall without being able to help you. Trouble is he didn't see who pushed you."

"I thought at the time it was Reston because he was so angry with me. And the way you spoke, I thought you didn't really believe he was innocent. But I can see now how Frank threw the matches in the cave to start a fire and distract attention while he pushed me." Bridget leaned back in her corner and closed her eyes, but she could not shut out the sight of that dark body silhouetted against the white cliff as it fell, could not shut out the sound of that thin screaming. Tears spilled down her cheeks.

"Bridget! Oh, God, Bridget! I didn't mean it. Don't cry, darling. Don't cry." Mike cursed because of the cast that pressed against her, so that he could not touch her.

"Let her alone," Keith called over his shoulder. "This isn't the time for tender dalliance."

There was a police car outside the Latham house when they arrived, and Jean came running out to the Cadillac. "We were just about crazy until the police came and said you were all right and—"

"Frank's dead," Bridget said dully.

"Yes, I know. When I think—"

"He's smashed up at the foot of the cliff. All smashed. He—" She staggered drunkenly and a policeman put Jean aside and lifted her easily in his arms, carried her into the house.

"Put her on the terrace," Jean said, and the policeman settled her on a lounge.

"Lie in the sun." Bridget began to cry.

II

"What put you onto the Snodgrass man in the first place?" the policeman asked Mike. They were all on the terrace except for Bridget, who slept in her darkened room as the result of a shot the doctor had given her.

"He claimed to be composing an opera, and he might as well have been working in a boiler factory with all that practicing going on. The thing was ridiculous."

"Of course!" Peg said. "Why didn't I see—but we were used to the noise. It took an outsider to think of it. And yet I believed in that opera."

"It had me stymied too," Mike admitted. "Last night my mother went down to the building where he used to live and talked to the superintendent and to a tenant who knew the Snodgrass family and—surprise, surprise! —is writing an opera on a relevant theme."

Peg groaned.

"Exactly. This composer used to talk to Frank's sister by the hour about it, claiming it had a wonderful role for her. So that testimony, plus the physical description Baxter got from the superintendent pretty well pinned down Frank's identity."

"Just who are you, anyhow, Mike?"

"He," Keith said proudly, "is the Michael Graves who wrote those excellent television plays: *The Third Man* and *Second Best* and *Exit Laughing.*"

Mike explained that he had agreed to look up Bridget Evans because of the conflicting accounts of her and how he had remained to look after her. "I could hardly have done worse. Peg doped her and put that hypodermic in her room and staged that shoplifting deal—those were fairly lousy things to do, Peg," he said mildly.

"I know. I'm sorry. Sorrier than I can say. I tried to make up in a way by nursing her, but I honestly believed she was lying, trying to throw suspicion on Jack for something she had done herself, and I was going to discredit her if I could. I couldn't see any other way to clear Jack."

"It never occurred to you that Bridget might be telling the truth as she saw it, even though her deductions were wrong?"

"No, she—acted guilty in a way. She didn't expect to be believed."

"There are reasons for that, reasons that go back to her childhood. I checked it out. Well, when Peg steered her out here and Frank insisted on coming along, I joined the party. For all the good I did. Frank nearly killed her with that dope. It was the sheerest chance he didn't get away with it. And then yesterday he tried to push us both off the cliff dwelling. And this morning—if that helicopter hadn't been able to keep you fellows informed of which way he was going—"

"It's a pity he took that way out," the policeman said. "He's one guy it would be a pleasure to pin a death sentence on. A real pleasure."

"You couldn't have done it. He was mad as a hatter. Bridget told me coming home. She'd have testified in his defense."

"She would!"

Mike nodded. "She thinks she's to blame for what he did, that she drove him to it."

"I suppose," Jean said, "he's the one who washed out those punch cups while the rest of us were scurrying around, getting in the way of the firemen and looking after that poor truck driver. You know, he's the very last person I'd have suspected. I thought he was infatuated with Bridget."

"He was. It made him feel guilty because it kept him postponing her murder."

"It's over now." Peg drew a deep breath.

"Unless Miss Evans wants to bring any charges," the policeman said. "It looks to me as though she could file suits against more than one of you folks. We'll talk to her tomorrow when she has recovered."

But Bridget did not want to bring any charge against anyone. She answered all the policeman's questions carefully, but it was apparent that her long rest had not done her as much good as it should. She was apathetic. She sat listlessly without moving or volunteering any comment, eating what was put before her. She listened to Peg's apologies without interest and to Jean's without comment. Only when Oliver came to sit beside her on the terrace did her voice break.

"Oh, Oliver!"

He took her hand and smiled at her. "It's all right, sweetie." He added in a kind of surprise. "Actually it is all right. I'll admit it was a kind of shock to watch eighty thousand go up in flames, but I felt like that guy in *A Tale of Two Cities,* 'It's a better thing I do. . . .' All right, laugh! I don't mind. And damned if it hasn't got me the first honest job offer I ever had. And all this time I've been blundering along with the idea that virtue was its only reward. Keith wants me to work on his ranch. Out of doors, a lot of riding. I told him he was a blasted fool to hire a thief and he just laughed. It's the kind of life I've always wanted. I couldn't have bought anything better with the money. And I think working might be fun."

He tightened his grasp of her hand. "Of course it would be more fun if I had you. Anyhow, you'll always know I'm the guy to whom you're worth your weight in gold." He bent over and kissed her. "I always knew you were going to be a jinx." He laughed and left her.

III

When the lights of Manhattan appeared below, Mike bent over to check Bridget's seat belt and awaken the sleeping girl.

"Home," he said. "We'll be landing in a few minutes." As she blinked at him he said, "It's all over, Bridget."

"It won't ever be over," she said somberly. "You know that. Louisa Snodgrass—Liz Conway—Frank—I killed them all. And Oliver's money went up in smoke to save my life. All because of me."

Mike made no comment until the bustle of landing was over, luggage had been retrieved, and a taxi was bearing them into Manhattan.

"When you are rested and have begun to think again, you will see how foolish all this is. You are guilty of only one thing and that is being a damned disturbing and dangerous woman. But that will be taken care of. I'm taking you out of circulation permanently." As she started to speak he said, "I know what I'm running into. You'll be trouble all your life but I'm the man who likes to live dangerously, so I am going to enjoy every minute of it."

At a stop light the taxi driver turned around, surveyed them both in a leisurely way, his eyes resting on the cast on Mike's arm. "You're sure a guy asking for trouble. Looks like you've already had it."

"That's probably just a beginning." Mike gave the address of his mother's apartment on Central Park West. "This will save her having to come and get you.

She is a very determined woman. Tomorrow you can talk to Lieutenant Baxter, and then you and I are going to be married."

"You're certainly going to look like a battered bridegroom."

"At least no one can deny I put up a real fight against you," he said and Bridget found herself laughing. With a little help from her, Mike found that his right arm was still useful.

GOTHIC MYSTERIES
of Romance
and Suspense . . .

by Rae Foley

A CALCULATED RISK
DARK INTENT
FATAL LADY
GIRL ON A HIGH WIRE
THE HUNDREDTH DOOR
MALICE DOMESTIC
THE MAN IN THE SHADOW
OMINOUS STAR
SCARED TO DEATH
THIS WOMAN WANTED
WILD NIGHT

and Velda Johnston

ALONG A DARK PATH
THE FACE IN THE SHADOWS
THE HOUSE ABOVE HOLLYWOOD
I CAME TO A CASTLE
THE LIGHT IN THE SWAMP
THE PEOPLE ON THE HILL
THE PHANTOM COTTAGE

Dell Books 75¢

*Biggest dictionary value
ever offered in paperback!*

The Dell paperback edition of

THE AMERICAN HERITAGE DICTIONARY
OF THE ENGLISH LANGUAGE

- Largest number of entries—55,000
- 832 pages—nearly 300 illustrations
- The only paperback dictionary with photographs

These special features make this new, modern dictionary clearly superior to any comparable paperback dictionary:

- More entries and more illustrations than any other paperback dictionary
- The first paperback dictionary with photographs
- Words defined in modern-day language that is clear and precise
- Over one hundred notes on usage with more factual information than any comparable paperback dictionary
- Unique appendix of Indo-European roots
- Authoritative definitions of new words from science and technology
- More than one hundred illustrative quotations from Shakespeare to Salinger, Spenser to Sontag
- Hundreds of geographic and biographical entries
- Pictures of all the Presidents of the United States
- Locator maps for all the countries of the world

A DELL BOOK 95c

If you cannot obtain copies of this title from your local bookseller, just send the price (plus 15c per copy for handling and postage) to Dell Books, Post Office Box 1000, Pinebrook, N. J. 07058.

How many of these Dell Bestsellers have you read?